THICKER THAN BLOOD II
THE
RAHSURRECTION

MARY A. FINLEY

McCurtain Press

Oklahoma Georgia

ACKNOWLEDGEMENTS

I give thanks to You, Most High, for bestowing upon me the ability to take blank pages and transform them into literary works. I dedicate this work to my beta readers: Terry Woods, Ruth Scribner-Kyle, Vonda Brooks, Leslie Hubbard and Bridgette Clemons. You ladies were honest and encouraging throughout this process. Thank you from the bottom of my heart.

Dr. Shelia Brown, my editor and dear friend, thanks so much, sistah. There are no words that suffice in expressing my love and gratitude to and for you. Maybe one day we'll see the Lamar family on the big screen.

*To my fans all over the world: Thanks be to God for you and your readership. I hope this sequel to **Thicker Than Blood** is as enjoyable and entertaining as the initial offering. You all give me much encouragement and support. I can't thank you enough!*

Mary Ann Finley is the founder and CEO of Mayrann Speaks Productions L.L.C. She's the author of *Corn Rowing Mama's Hair on a Sunday, Somebody Say Grace and Thicker Than Blood (vol.1).* She is the publisher of McCurtain Press and lives in Stone Mountain, Georgia area.

THICKER THAN BLOOD
II
THE RAHSURRECTION

Mary A. Finley

PROLOGUE

December 2012

A lean, statuesque gentleman towers over a double headstone with his head bowed. He views the epitaph and the moaning within him releases, as if he's seeking solace from their spirits. *I let you down so many times. You took me in, gave me your name, raised me as blood-kin, and I let you down.* He drags his feet over to the right of his parents' graves. The wind blows through his trench coat, yet the chill he has isn't from the biting temperature, but the stark reality that he is dead. Dead to his family. Dead to his old gangster buddies. Dead to the world as he once knew it. He's been chiseled onto a headstone for over nine years and views it now for the first time. *I have to make this right.*

He takes a long breath, exhales and steps to the next grave on the right. The dirt is fresh, and a generic headstone marks its tenant. He unbuttons his coat. His legs betray him, as emotions he has kept hidden since first hearing of her death finally surface. He kneels. "I'm so sorry. You have to know I never meant for this to happen to you . . . you of all people. Everything I did I thought was for your good. Please forgive me." He reaches in his pocket, retrieves a handkerchief to wipe his face and whispers, "I'll make this right." His whole body quivers. "I promise on your grave, my sweet baby girl, I will make this right."

PART ONE

TROUBLE IN MY WAY

Chapter One

Three months earlier

"Where in God's name have you been?' The veins in Gerald Lamar's neck look like they're about to explode. "I've been calling all over Dallas going crazy looking for you, and you waltz in here at 2:30 AM like it's no big deal. Have you forgotten there's a man out there who's threatened to kill us? And where the hell is my son!"

"Your son?" His wife, Bridget, stands up so abruptly her chair falls to the floor. "I'm surprised you noticed he wasn't here, and more surprised you noticed I wasn't here."

Gerald picks up the chair and slams it back upright. "What the fuck are you talking about?"

The scowl on his face pushes Bridget over the top. "How dare you use that language with me? You save the profanity for when you hang out with ya brother, hear? I will not be cussed at in my own home. I've never done that to you. And what I'm talking about is you. I don't know where my husband is anymore. You come home every night, okay, and that's great, but you're not here. All you do is throw dinner down your throat, shower and head to your office, where you keep your head buried in church business."

Gerald turns around and heads upstairs.

Bridget throws up both hands. "Yeah, run away, 'good Reverend Dr.' That's all you ever do lately. Keep avoiding your issues like they'll automatically disappear." She pulls a pitcher out of the refrigerator, pours a glass of lemonade, rolls her eyes, sits at the table and starts sipping.

Gerald stops in his tracks, and then moves slowly back down the stairs. He approaches Bridget from behind, puts his brawny arms around her and plants a soft kiss on her neck.

"That won't work this time, sweetie," Bridget says.

Gerald sits down and she looks him over. "Why are you still in your street clothes?"

He clasps his hands and responds in a calmer voice tone. "Because I was getting ready to drive to the police station and report my wife and son missing. Baby, you didn't even answer your phone." Gerald sighs. "I'm sorry, okay? Sorry for yelling and cussing. Sorry for working too hard. Sorry for whatever else I need to be sorry for, but please don't ever do this again. Your body guard said you gave him the slip around midnight. I thought I was gonna lose you." He covers her hands with his. "When will you understand—I'm nothing without you?"

Bridget stands, reaches her arms out for him, and they hold one another without speaking for a few minutes. She kisses the top of his bald-head.

Gerald looks up at with her with a sheepish grin. "Does that mean this fight is over? It's been a minute since we had words like this. I don't like it at all."

Bridget cups Gerald's face with her hands. "Baby, listen. I want you back; where did *you* go? Lately you've been somebody different and don't realize it. You convinced your whole family to move back here when you accepted that position at Narrow Way Baptist. I even agreed to move onto this estate where you grew up. This old mansion drives me nuts sometimes." She kisses him on the lips.

"I know. I'm so grateful; you're my angel," Gerald whispers, and slowly caresses her back.

"Well, my place is with my husband, who is supposed to be my number one protector. Lately I feel like"—her voice cracks—"your last priority, so does Marcus. When we adopted him you were so proud that your face lit up every time you saw him; now in his senior year he can't get 30 minutes of your time without your cell ringing every 10 minutes? The Lord's not calling you to minister to everybody except your family."

Gerald pulls Bridget closer, lays his head on her chest and rocks from side to side while listening to her heartbeat. "I'm under so much pressure, sweetheart."

"Baby, please don't forget, I'm under with you. That's all I'm asking."

Gerald looks up at her again, wipes her tear-stained cheeks with his thumbs and slightly brushes her lips with his. "I'll do better, promise." He kisses her from her neck down to the top of her breasts.

She arches her back and moans. He unbuttons her blouse, removes it and her bra, then takes one of her full nipples in his mouth. Her breathing gets heavier. She closes her eyes. "Gerald," she whispers, in a sultry alto-voice he hasn't heard in a while.

The more he sucks the more Bridget feels her sweet-spot moisten. "Gerald, baby . . . oh . . . oh . . . Jesus." Within minutes she's completely naked, and he's rubbing every one of the soft full-figured curves he loves so much. When he opens his legs wider and pulls her closer, she reaches down and massages his firm manhood.

Gerald groans. "I need you." He stands, pushes her up against the kitchen wall and looks into her eyes. "Jet, I love you so much. Don't ever think that's not true." He begins licking her nipples, her belly; then kneels on both knees, finally reaching his goldmine. Bridget grabs his head and her eyes roll back. "Gerald, baby, don't please don't . . . stop. It's been too long. Oh, my . . . God, it's so good, oh oh . . . sweetie!"

He props her thighs up on his broad shoulders to steady her, and keeps working his tongue until her gyrations get out of control.

Bridget thrusts her pelvis forward one last time, and then speaks in a language only the two of them understand.

Chapter Two

"Shirley, Shirley!" Tip Collier pushes the panic button on the side of Shirley Sinclair's hospital bed and a nurse rushes in. He tells her, "She was talking to me one minute and then she stopped breathing."

A doctor and two more nurses enter the room. Tip picks his sleeping son up and backs into a corner while they tend to Shirley. Little Tip squirms in his arms. "Mommy! Daddy, what are they doing to her?" He screams, "Let me go. I wanna get back in bed with mommy."

Tip kisses the seven year old on his forehead, and holds him as tight as he can, then pushes the door open to go out into the hall. One of the corrections officers stands and offers his seat. Momentarily bereft of words to console his son, Tip sits and rocks him back and forth. His neck and shirt collar soon become damp from Little Tip's tears.

Three days later a private graveside service is held; Tip, his son, and Shirley's Aunt Maggie are the only people present. They bury her next to her parents.

When Tip arrives back in Dallas the next morning the local media is all abuzz of the drama that happened at his brother's church. Gerald calls a special meeting of the trustees, staff, and security before the morning service starts. He sits at the head of the conference room table, with Tip seated beside him.

"Ladies and gentlemen," Tip says, "good morning, and thank you for giving up an extra half-hour of your day so we can touch base again on what has and is to occur here. As we all know, former trustee chairperson, Calvin Wells, was arrested this past Tuesday for embezzlement of close to $70,000 from the church accounts." He leans forward with his elbows on the table. "We have video as well as bank records as proof. He did make bail, so let's be clear: Mr. Wells is no longer welcome on this campus for any reason, and if spotted must be promptly reported to security." He turns to Gerald. "Pastor?"

Gerald clears his throat and looks at the faces of each person in the room. He presses his fingertips on the table as he speaks. "Now, it's good to be careful, but I'm not fearful. There is nothing that can separate us from the love of God, amen? As the leaders of this congregation I'm counting on all of us in this circle to be examples to the rest of the members, and move forward in God's grace. He is our fence of protection every day. Let's not allow the enemy to hinder our worship and praise." 'Amen' rings throughout the room.

"As head of security," Tip continues, "I'll be present at all services, including Wednesday nights, and there will be two guards on all doors for an indefinite period of time—that's both inside and outside doors. Wells has threatened the pastor's life and we take that with utmost seriousness." Heads all over the room give an affirmative nod.

"All right," Gerald says, "let's be vigilant yet offer sincere honor to the Lord today. I believe everything will be fine. This meeting is adjourned."

Gerald escorts his staff to the door and shuts it, then addresses Tip. "I'm glad you two made it back safely from Georgia. Hate to hear about Little Tip being in such grief. I mean that from the bottom of my heart. You know that, right?"

Tip walks over to Gerald. "Yeah, I know, but if you had bee—"

"Not this morning, okay? Let's just get through these two services today. You got my back?"

Tip punches Gerald on the shoulder. "Your front and your back, Negro. Don't ever doubt that. You put on a good face for others but I see your trepidation, G. You can't fool me."

"You know what else I know?" Gerald steps back and looks at Tip. "I got the 'blue cheese' for head of security." He chuckles. "I'm just sayin', my brother, your shoes probably cost more than Wells stole."

"Man, hush and go pontificate." Tip and Gerald laugh as they head into the sanctuary.

"Mr. Collier, Mr. Collier."

Tip slowly opens one eye and quickly shuts it after seeing his squeaky-voiced administrative assistant staring in his face.

"I saw you open that eye, Mr. Collier; you ain't slick." Sonya puts one hand on her hip and shakes Tip's shoulder with the other.

He opens both eyes, and gives her a look that could kill. "Sonya, good Monday morning. Is there a reason you're interrupting me and 'Jilly from Philly?"

Sonya giggles. "Huh, Jill Scott wouldn't give your little butt the time of day. And you need to stop falling asleep in your office with ya head all cocked back, snoring. You know that does not look professional."

Tip leans forward like he's getting up, and instead lays his head on his desk. "Sonya, I've told you a million times, there ain't but one boss here. This is my office, my suite, and even if I want to lie down on the got-damn floor and slobber like a baby that's no one's business but mine."

"Well I sure hope to never come in and see that," Sonya retorts. "Anyway you have a phone call."

"You could've buzzed me."

"I did, but all I heard was snoring." She giggles again.

"Take a message."

18

"All right, but it's somebody from the Georgia State Penitentiary." Sonya walks toward the door.

Tip sits up. "What? Was it a collect call?" He realizes how silly that question is, given that Shirley is dead, and lays his head back down.

"No, it is not collect. She said she was the family something liaison or whatever. Will you please just pick up line one before she hangs up." Sonya sashays her voluptuous bottom out of his office and slams the door behind her.

Tip stands and stretches before hitting the flashing light on his desk phone. "Good morning, Patrick Collier speaking, Ms. Drexler. What can I do for you? We just spoke Saturday."

"Good morning, Mr. Collier, I'm just touching base to see how you and your son are. That's a part of my job. Can't close the case until I do two follow-ups."

"Nothing has changed in two days. It'll take some time for our son to come to grips with never seeing his mom again; he'll be fine eventually."

"I do hope so. Oh, by the way, Shirley's father's been calling me this past week. I didn't know if you wanted to give him the bad news or if we should intervene. It's really your call since you're her son's legal guardian."

Tip sits down, and picks up the receiver. "You must be mistaken; both of her parents are deceased. Her father died right after her 18th birthday." He yawns. "I don't know who is calling you, but it's not him."

Ms. Drexler is silent for a moment. "Um, are you sure, because he's been coming to see her for about, oh . . . six years now. She seemed happy to have his company. He cleared fed and state guidelines and was approved as a visitor, let me see . . . yeah, here it is—July 10, 2005."

Tip holds the receiver out and looks at it, then speaks into it again. "Look, the only father I ever knew Shirley had is who we buried her next to this past weekend. This might be one of her old lovers or something but he's not her father."

"I don't mean to upset you, sir. You're probably right if she never told you about him. I'll let him know when he calls back that she's deceased. Sorry for the inconvenience. Good day to you."

Tip puts the receiver back in its cradle. "What the hell was that?" He pulls a liquor bottle from his desk drawer, takes a sip, resumes his reclining position and closes his eyes again. "Put that loony bitch in the grave and she still bringing me unnecessary drama."

Chapter Three

Celeste Lamar's three year old daughter, Lia, runs full speed into their kitchen. "Mommy," she shouts, and jumps up and down in front of Celeste. Agnes, her nanny—a lovely, plump, gray-haired Caucasian lady, is right on her heels.

"Young lady, we don't run in this house, and you know that." She shakes her index finger at Lia. "Your mother's no doubt had a long day, you hear me?" She smiles and winks at Celeste. "I'm sorry, she had a rather exciting afternoon at the zoo."

"Oh that's all right," Celeste responds, while picking up her daughter. "I'm just as glad to see her and you. You're right, this has been one hectic day." Celeste gives her daughter a kiss on each cheek. "You know I've already had my nose in the pots, Agnes. I couldn't help it. That roast was calling my name as soon as I walked through the door."

Agnes blushes. "Oh, thank you. I'll get Lia washed up and settled in the play room while you relax and get ready for dinner. Is Mr. Faber joining us this evening?"

"Yes, I am." Landis' announcement surprises everyone.

"Daddy!" Lia jumps in her father's arms.

"Now that's the kind of welcome I expect to get when I come home. My little girl still loves me, no matter what?"

"No matter what!" Lia pouts her lips for her father to land a kiss on, and he obliges.

Landis and Celeste greet one another with a brush-of-the-cheek kiss.

Agnes raises one eyebrow, then tells Lia, "Let's go on to play, okay? Your mom and dad have to wash up and get ready for dinner." She takes the child's hand and leads her out of the room.

Celeste peers daggers at Landis. "So you finally decided having dinner with us was important?"

"How the hell you gonna start this shit as soon as I get in the door? I'm so tired of your insinuations." He loosens his tie. "Why should I come home every day if all you're gonna to do is bitch?"

"Fuck you too," Celeste replies. "That hot-pink envelope laying on the table, with the even hotter pink panties inside, is for you." She folds her arms and leans up against the marble kitchen counter. "You haven't played pro ball in three years. I'd appreciate it if you tell your little groupie hoes to stop addressing mail to our home. Lia could've saw it and thought it was something pretty to play with."

"I don't want to play your game today, baby. Going upstairs to shower."

"This is not a game. Look at the fucking letter." Celeste picks it up and throws it in his face. He ignores her, and heads for the stairwell.

Trey Lamar hits 2 on his speed-dial and gets an answer after the first ring.

"Collier and Associates, this is Sonya speaking."

He pulls up the recliner lever on the side of his easy-chair. "I'd like to make an appointment to see you buck-naked in my bedroom in say . . . two hours. You got some availability?"

Sonya beams and lowers her voice. "Well that depends. Do I need to bring anything?"

"Nope." Trey unhooks the tie around his hair and lets his locs fall freely onto his shoulders. "Just you. You're everything I need."

Sonya pulls up into Trey's driveway around 7 PM. When she rings the doorbell, he answers dressed in all white cotton, with his shirt unbuttoned. His dreads glisten in the orange rays of sunset coming through his door. Sonya leans up against the doorway to keep her balance.

Trey steps back to admire her curves. She has on a candy-apple red strapless mini dress, that leaves nothing to the imagination. He pulls her into his arms and closes the door. "Whew, damn, 'Chocolate Thunder', you trying to convince me to have dessert before dinner?" They give each other a lingering kiss.

"Wait," Sonya says, "what do you mean dinner? I thought this was all about dessert tonight."

Trey grabs her purse and keys, lays them on the small table in his foyer, then stands behind her with his hands over her eyes. He guides her into his main dining room. When he removes his hands,

Sonya grins from ear to ear. There's a full-course meal, crystal, china and vanilla candles on the table. She turns around and wraps her arms around his waist.

"Oh, sweetie, what is all this for? You didn't have to do this!"

Trey leads her to the head of the table, pulls out her chair, then sits in the one next to her. He takes her hands and kisses them. "Sonya, first of all, don't panic." He chuckles. "We've both come to the conclusion that marriage is out of the question until you finish law school, and I'm so proud of you for pursuing that dream. So I'm not about to pop a proposal on you, ebony beauty."

Sonya lets out a deep breath. "Thank goodness. You had me nervous for a minute." She's curious about the serious look on Trey's face.

"Baby," Trey says.

Sonya raises her eyebrows. "What?"

He presses his lips against hers for a few seconds, then pulls an oblong case from the chair on the other side of his. He opens it and Sonya blinks, with her mouth agape.

"I love you, and I'm in love with you. Felt this way since I walked into Uncle Tip's office two years ago, and saw you sitting there like you ran the world. Baby, I love you, never met a woman that makes me feel the way you do."

As she continues to stare at him, he takes the pearls out of the box, fastens them around her neck, then traces her face with his finger.

With tears dripping down her cheeks, Sonya gets out of her chair and sits straddled on Trey's lap. "I love you too." She kisses his face all over, and finally stops at his lips.

After a kiss long enough to almost break the *Guinness Book of World Records,* Trey whispers, "I know you feel that."

Sonya nods. "Mm hmm, looks like we better blow these candles out and cover this food because we're definitely having dessert first."

Around 2 AM Trey's cell phone rings. He unwraps his body from the hold Sonya has on him and checks to make sure she's sound asleep, then answers the phone whispering. "Tracy, I told you not to call me tonight . . . What do you mean I stood you up the other day; you know we don't roll like that . . . No I'm not saying you're just a booty call but, hold on a minute, okay?" He puts his boxers back on, moves quietly into the bathroom and shuts the door.

After about 15 minutes he comes out to find Sonya standing there, fully dressed with her purse on her shoulder and keys in her hand.

"Sonya, baby, where are you going? I thought you were spending the night."

She looks at him for a few more seconds then turns and marches all the way to the front door, with him trailing her and calling her name. She makes an about-face and exhales to stop any tears from showing up, then puts her hand on Trey's face, and gives him one quick kiss.

"Trey, when I said I love you, I meant it. Thought you meant it too. That's why I went all against my standards and gave you my body after only dating 2 months."

"Sonya, of course I do, what's wrong? That phone call? Babe, she don't mean nothing to me, it's not even like th—"

Sonya puts her index finger on his lips. "You've said a lot tonight, now it's my turn." She sighs. "You're one of the most mature 29 year old men I've ever met; yet you're also still too young in so many of your ways.

"I don't know why you feel the need to string all these other women along, but baby, you're in love with a grown ass woman." She grabs his hand and puts the necklace in it. "When you get through playing house and patty-cake with your little girlfriends, bring me back my pearls—no time sooner."

Trey stands in the doorway with a look of contrition as Sonya gets in her car. After she drives off, he signals his bodyguard to follow her. When he turns to go back inside, an explosion rocks his house like an earthquake.

Chapter Four

Trey sits on his oversized couch with Bridget on his right and Gerald on the left. Every sound around him seems far away. He looks up and sees a uniformed police detective pointing at a small notebook with a short pencil, saying something; however, Trey can't make out what. He bows his head and stares at the string of pearls in his hand.

Gerald massages Trey's shoulders. "Listen," he says. "If you don't feel like answering questions right now, you don't have to. I'll take you down to the station later."

Trey is relieved to hear his father's voice. "No, dad, it's okay." He turns to the detective. "What is it you're saying? Please repeat that."

"Mr. Lamar, I'm very sorry for your loss, sir. We just have a few questions." The officer flips the notepad back to the first page. "It looks like the fire department was able to extinguish all fires, even the damage to your roof; you'll want to get that fixed as soon as possible. We found the sunroof glass in one of the rooms on the second story. It crashed through a window. That's the extent of the damage to your house."

Trey gives the officer an agitated look. "Man, I don't give a damn about this house; I can buy a new one tomorrow. You're sitting here talking about a got-damn house. How about my precious baby? Did you write down the details of her damages? The suns up now. Shouldn't ya'll be out scouring my estate for fragments of . . . her beautiful . . . body." Trey lowers his head again and moans. Bridget wraps her arms around him.

"Sir, I'm sorry, I was trying to ease into those quest—"

Trey erupts. "Ask the damn questions that matter or get the fuck out my house!" His hands tremble so much he almost drops the pearls.

"Okay, Mr. Lamar. I understand. We're here to help. Our goal is to find out who the perpetrator is."

Trey raises his bloodshot eyes and glares at the cop. "I doubt very seriously you understand the love of your life being blown to pieces in your driveway. You got five minutes."

"What was your relationship with Ms. Collins?"

"She was my soul-mate," Trey answers. "I just wish I had realized that before now."

"How long was she here last night, sir?"

Trey closes his eyes. "She came around 7-7:30, and we said goodnight around 2:30AM. That's when I saw her get into her Jag and drive off . . . for the last time."

The detective writes on his pad. "Was there anyone else on the property that you know of?"

"Yes, my bodyguard, Walt."

"Would that be the gentleman over there—Walter Clements?" He nods his head toward the corner of the room, where a Dwayne Johnson look-a-like stands with his massive arms folded.

"Yes, he usually comes on duty around 10 o'clock."

"I take it you trust Mr. Clements." The detective looks over at Walt.

Trey answers, "With my life, we've had one another's backs since high school."

"So you're saying from approximately 7-10 PM you and Ms. Collins were the only people on the property. She gave no indication of something being wrong with her car, yet when she was leaving, her vehicle detonated? Do you know of anyone who would want to do harm to the victim?"

Trey shakes his head. "Sonya was kind, caring and always full of jokes. I don't see why anyone would do that to her." He looks at the ceiling.

"What about you?"

Trey squints his eyes at the detective. "What about me?"

"There is a possibility whoever planted that device thought the vehicle belonged to you."

The tone of the officer's voice is too matter-of-fact for Trey. "Man, go straight to hell. You trying to say I'm the cause of my baby's murder? It's time for ya'll to vacate my premises!"

"Wait a minute," Gerald interjects. "As a former detective, I know this is standard procedure, but do you know what happened at my church last week?"

"Yes, Dr. Lamar, we're quite aware; we'll be bringing Mr. Wells in for questioning once we get back to the station. He's definitely a prime suspect."

Celeste stomps into the room. "Then why are you still here? Detective Lowe, are you interrogating my brother as a suspect too?"

"Counselor, you know the routine. The last person who saw the victim alive gets interviewed first." Detective Lowe and Celeste stare at one another. Celeste reaches into her jeans' pocket and hands him a card.

"As you already know, Trey's not only my brother, he's my business partner, and as of right now, distraught client. Don't you see the condition he's in? If you have any more questions, we'll come down to headquarters." She purses her lips. "Good day, gentlemen."

Once the officers leave, Gerald stands and opens his arms to his son. Trey gets up quickly, embraces his father and lays his head on his shoulder. He allows the first tear to break free, then the rest flow like a quiet river stream. Bridget and Celeste join their embrace.

Chapter Five

Tip saunters through his front door and the aroma is so heavenly he licks his lips. "Mama, you in the kitchen?"

Claudette pours cake mix into two round pans. "Patrick, you come in here every day at almost the same time, and asks me the same question. Why?"

He kisses her on the cheek. "Because I smell all that love up in here, pretty lady." He tries to stick his finger into one of the cake pans and she smacks his hand.

"You know better," his salt-n-pepper haired mother says. "How was Sonya's memorial? Did Trey come?"

Tip pulls a stool from under the kitchen island, sits down, and takes off his shades. "Heart wrenching, you know? She was like my daughter."

Claudette puts the pans in the oven, wipes her hands, walks over to Tip and gives him a hug. "I know you're gonna miss her, dear, but she's doing better than us now. Somebody told me Gerald gave a lovely eulogy."

"Yeah, he did his thing, and Trey was there. Never said a word, but he was there. Guess who finally convinced him to come out of the house."

Claudette puts a couple of rolls on a saucer and places it in front of him. "Don't have to guess. It's about time she decided she was still a mother. No matter how much our children say or think they hate us, one thing I know: they all want their mothers."

Tip chuckles. "Yes, Camilla will be here for a couple of weeks. Mama, how you find out things before I do? Just nosey." He bites into a roll.

"Never mind that," Claudette says. She waves him off and leaves the kitchen. When she returns she lays a small toolbox on the island.

"Was picking up my grandbaby's room today, and found something you ought to see."

Tip sighs. "We have a maid, ma'am. How many times do I have to tell you that?"

"About as many times as I tell you it don't matter, now look in the toolbox." Claudette pulls out the stool beside him and sits.

Tip opens the lid on the box. "All I see in here are his play-tools. Am I missing something?"

His mother raises the top tool tray up and removes the toys from bottom one.

Tip furrows his brow as he picks up five small envelops from the bottom of the container; each one has either Little Tip's birthday or 'Christmas' written on it. They all contain two hundred-dollar bills. He looks over at Claudette. "What the hell?"

"Listen, baby, " Claudette says. "When you ask him about this, please, just be calm."

Little Tip leans up against his grandmother's lap, fumbling with a Kleenex in his hands. Claudette gently rubs the boy's sandy colored hair he inherited from Tip's Creole father. Tears well in Little Tip's eyes. "I don't wanna get a spanking, daddy."

Tip squats and gets eye-to-eye with his son. "Little man, dad's not going to punish you at all. Tell me where you got all this money."

Little Tip sniffles. "It's suppose to be just a secret between us."

"Us who, son?'

"Me and mommy. She said he gave it to me for her because she didn't have any presents for me, and she felt bad. I didn't want to keep a secret from you, daddy, but she made me promise and . . . and you said a person should never go back on their promise. Mommy said it would make you mad." He wipes his eyes with the Kleenex. "He was always nice to me."

Tip stands and picks Little Tip up. He kisses the boy's forehead. "You stop crying, all right. I've never hit you, and never will. Sometimes when grownups get angry with one another they say things they shouldn't; your mommy and I did that sometimes too. But remember I told you that was wrong and we never should've done that in front of you?"

Little Tip shakes his head up and down. "Yes, sir, and ya'll stopped doing it."

Tip sits on the couch with his son on his lap. "You miss her and I know it's hard. Shirley's in heaven now, okay, so tell me who the man was that gave you the money."

"Mommy said he was my granddaddy. He had gray hair, and would come into our Sunday School class and give me a hug and a envelope on Christmas and my birthday. But I guess I won't get one for this Christmas." Tip and Claudette look at one another.

"Honeybunch," Claudette says, "who is the man you're talking about? Is he a member of our church?"

"Yes, ma'am." He looks up at Tip. "You remember, daddy, when he was on TV and the police put them cuffs on his hands, and he said terrible things to Uncle Gerald?" Little Tip shakes his head back and forth. "I never want to see that man again."

Chapter Six

Bridget plops down on the sofa in her living room, kicks off her stilettos and taps her Bluetooth. "Hold on a minute, sweetie." She tosses her suit jacket to the side and starts flipping through the mail. A plain white envelope with no return address or postage on it catches her attention. She opens it and her mouth drops. She forgets her step-son is on the other end of the phone.

Trey taps the window in his limo to signal the chauffeur he's ready to leave his office parking lot. "What's up, auntie, you all right?"

Bridget holds her breath for a second, then puts the letter down on the couch beside her. She answers, trying to veil her emotions. "Trey, don't go home."

"What, why?"

"Don't ask questions, just do as I say, hear me? Please call Celeste and tell her to get here as soon as possible too. I have to call your dad." She hangs up and dials the church's number.

About 20 minutes later the adults in the family meet in Gerald's home-office. Little Tip and Lia are upstairs watching television, being attended by Claudette and Walt; Bridget sits between Marcus and Trey on the couch, holding their hands; Celeste and Landis are hugged up on the loveseat; Tip leans against the arm of the sofa, dressed in Italian everything, with his hands and feet crossed.

Detective Lowe unfolds the note and sees it was put together using different letters cut and pasted from various magazines. He reads, *"Tell Trey he's next."*

Trey takes a deep breath and Bridget intertwines her fingers in his. "That mofo better stay the hell away from me," he whispers.

"Has anyone touched this besides you and your wife," Detective Lowe asks Gerald.

"No, I read it to my family and held on to it until you arrived."

"Good, we'll check for fingerprints, but I doubt anyone who would write a note like this would be stupid enough to leave any."

Gerald paces back and forth. "So now will you take that threat Wells made seriously?" He punches his palm with his fist. "The man is out there stalking my family, now he's naming who he's targeting next? Somehow he got, or got someone else, close enough to our house to slip that into our mailbox."

Detective Lowe removes his bifocals. "You know as well as I do, this note isn't adequate evidence to accuse Wells of anything. Of course we'll request he come in and be interrogated again, but same as when we questioned him about Ms. Collins' murder—all we have is speculation."

Tip stands, puts his hand in his pockets, and walks over to Lowe. "You know what, you're 100% correct. Let me tell you what isn't speculation: that bastard approached my son at church several times during the past two years, perpetrated as his grandfather, gave him money and told him never to tell me."

"What!" Bridget and Celeste ask in unison. They both jump up from their seats. Gerald looks at Tip concerned because it's been years since he's seen his brother's green eyes look so menacing. A memory of their father flashes in his mind.

They all stare at Tip in disbelief as he repeats what his son told him and Claudette the day before. When he finishes, he gives the police officers a gaze as cold as icebergs. "I'm trying not to revert back to my old ways, but if you don't bring him in, best believe, I will. There won't be a fucking thing pretty about it. That's not a threat; that's a fact."

Chapter Seven

Benjamin Mackey stares at his petite wife, Jacqueline, from across the breakfast table, with a twinkle in his hazel eyes. "Come on, you know they're good."

Jacqueline sticks a fork full of chocolate-chip pancakes in her mouth and chews without any expression on her face. She swallows then takes a sip of orange juice.

Benjamin grins. "Well?"

"Honey, I'll tell you this much," Jacqueline says, "they have improved over the past two years, since we got married. Keep practicing."

"Daddy, I think they're delicious!" His four year old step-daughter, Marissa says, with a mouth full of food.

He leans over and kisses her on the cheek. "I know they are, cherry blossom. Your mom's just an ole meanie." He winks at Jacqueline.

"Baby, you know I appreciate any time you make a meal." She gets up, walks over to him and kisses his lips.

Marissa turns up her nose. "Why all that mushy stuff all the time. That's all you two do."

Benjamin bursts out laughing, picks her up and showers her face with kisses. She giggles. "Do it again, again."

"No, baby, we have to go so we won't be late." Jacqueline glances up at Benjamin, while tying Marissa's shoelaces. "You could come to church with us every once in a while."

Benjamin starts clearing the table and shakes his head. "Must we have this conversation every Sunday? I told you Sunday is my day of rest. Hell, it's my only off day, and the last thing I want to do is spend two hours of it listening to some country Florida preacher tell me how close I am to hell."

Once Jacqueline and Marissa leave, Benjamin grabs his plate, rushes into the living room and turns the TV on to his favorite church service. He listens attentively to every word the pastor says. Today the pastor has an intense look on his face and grips the sides of the pulpit.

"*First of all,*" Gerald says, "*I ask that we all remember the family of Sister Sonya Collins in prayer as they grieve. Her death was untimely and this morning, church, my heart is so heavy for her parents, because there is no mourning like that of a parent who loses a child. She was a lovely young lady, inside and out. Her memorial last Friday was a celebration of life.*

"*Secondly, I won't tarry here long, but if anyone has been keeping an ear out to the local news, you know the man police suspect did this evil act has threatened my family more than once, and is now on the run.*

"*The Dallas Police Department has an all points bulletin out for Calvin Wells, our former head-trustee. I ask that you please pray fervently for my family, and our church family.*

"*Forgive me, saints, but . . . this morning I need to hear a word from the Lord myself. I've asked our assistant pastor to bring the message today. After the choir sings a number, please open your ears and hearts to what God has to say through this woman of God.*"

When Jacqueline comes home that afternoon, she finds a handwritten note from Benjamin on the kitchen table. As she reads it her knees buckle, her heart begins to race and she has to sit down. All it says is he's left the state of Florida on an important personal mission, and doesn't know when or if he'll return.

PART TWO

<u>A SHADOW IN THE</u>

<u>DARK</u>

Chapter Eight

Wells sits with his back up against the headboard of the bed in a roach-motel just outside of Tulsa. He has no idea what time it is, just that it's dark, and he's spent the last day and a half dodging law enforcement. He takes a drink from a bottle of whiskey he's been nursing for over an hour, throws the TV remote across the room and grips the pistol under his blanket. "How the hell would I kill anybody with my hands shaking like this?"

He falls asleep in the same upright position. Around dawn the liquor bottle slips from his hand and hits the floor with a thud. Wells' eyes pop wide open at the smell of an expensive cigar. There's someone sitting in the chair directly across from his bed. He can't see the man's face because the only light in the room is a stream coming in from the streetlight. The man's outline in the shadows looks huge. Wells throws the covers back and feels for his gun.

"Is this what you looking for?" Benjamin asks, holding up the weapon.

Wells darts his eyes over to the door.

"Try it if you want to, son-of-a-bitch. Your head will be blown off before you take a second step."

"Li- listen, I don't have nothing of value. Please, j-just don't kill me."

Benjamin laughs maniacally. "You think I'm here to rob you?" He crosses his legs and blows a puff of smoke into the darkness. "You don't have anything I want but information."

Wells reaches his hand toward Benjamin for a shake. "My, my name is Wells, Calvin Wells."

Benjamin doesn't move. "Keep your distance. I knew who you were the second I saw your ugly ass mug-shot plastered on the news."

"Who are you? I know your voice from somewhere. How did you find me? Did Gerald send you; are you working for him?"

"I found you because your ass is still as dumb as a damn rock, and running to the same spots when cops turn up the heat,"

Benjamin answers. "No, I don't work for the good pastor, but I'm deeply indebted to him. Gonna start paying him back right now. For the sake of this conversation, call me 'Blackula'. Now, why the fuck are you after him and his family?"

Wells stammers, "No, no, no, you got it all wrong. I haven't done nothing to him, well, except steal money from the church. The girl that got killed, I didn't do that." He straightens his back up against the headboard and closes his eyes. "I'm not a murderer."

"Just a thief, and still a chicken-shit coward." Benjamin puts his cigar out on the coffee table beside him, then puts the gun in his lap. "Start from the beginning, and don't miss a beat."

Wells starts fast-talking. "Okay, okay, I used to launder money for Gerald's brother—one of the most notorious drug lords in Georgia history—until he got killed. After that I laid low and tried to go legit, but it was no use." He closes his eyes and shakes his head. "Lost everything: my wife, children, house . . . just went bankrupt."

"Bitch, do I look like Damien Escobar to you? I'm not here to play violins. Weak ass. Get to the point."

"All right, one day, about two years ago, I got a call from this man, who sounded as old as dirt. He kept coughing so much I thought he was gonna strangle himself to death. He said I had the right reputation for a job he needed done, and offered to set me up if I moved to Dallas. Told me all I had to do was keep an eye on Tip's son."

"Keep going."

"He only paid my shelter expenses so I was still broke all the time. That's when I joined Gerald's church, and stayed so close to him, got to looking like his right-hand man. Even lied about being a top-notch accountant and showed him my fabricated credentials. Knew they would clear when he checked 'em, 'cause I still got some pretty good underground connections."

"Dishonor among thieves. Finish the story, fool."

Wells smirks. "Gerald trusted me enough to appoint me as chairman of the trustees. Thought I was gonna bust a gut." He snickers. "That was too easy, so you know, I did what I do—rigged the books a little at a time. It was all good until he hired Tip as head of security." Wells turns up his face like there's a stench in the air. "Can't stand that arrogant asshole."

Benjamin strikes a match to re-light his cigar and Wells gets a quick glimpse of his face. He still can't recall who he is. "Who is your boss?"

"See, that's the craziest shit about all of this. We never met in person. I just always got checks in the mail for my bills. He called me for reports and when he wanted something extra done, like giving Tip's son money and saying it was from his mother. I never figured that out."

Benjamin stands. "What's his name? Tell me right now and you might not die before I leave."

"I don't know, man, for real. If I had known his plans included blowing people up and shit, I never woulda agreed to the arrangement! Please, don't kill me. I'll do whatever you wa—"

Benjamin is up in Wells' face with the gun in no time flat. He turns on the lamp by the bed, and gives him a crooked smile.

Wells hollers, and tries to leap over to the other side of the bed.

"What's up, old running buddy?" Benjamin puts the gun to Wells' head and whispers in his ear. "Long time no see."

Wells swallows hard and begins hyperventilating. "Y-y-you're dead. It can't be. You're dead!"

Benjamin cocks the pistol. "I'm a vampire remember, motherfucker? We live forever. Now, before I pull this trigger and put you out of your misery, give me a name."

Gerald pushes the volume up on his car's Bluetooth to hear Detective Lowe clearer. "Did you say what I think you said?"

"Yes, sir," Lowe responds. We gotta a call from the Tulsa County Sherriff's Department. Wells was found dead this morning around 11 o'clock, in a sleazy motel out on I-44. The serial number had been removed from the pistol in his hand, but his prints were the only ones on it. Looks like suicide."

After Lowe hangs up, Gerald leans back in his seat and allows his body to relax."Thank you, Most High," he whispers.

Chapter Nine

That night Benjamin disguises himself and checks into one of the high-end hotels off Dallas' North Stemmons Freeway. When he was there three years ago, the bustling hotel was a good place to hide in plain sight. After getting little sleep, he lies in bed the next morning, looking up at the ceiling. *This is risky, but I have to stay close if I'm going to keep the family safe. Wells didn't know shit, not even that old rat-bastard's name. Plus, why was he giving Tip's son money? This doesn't add up.*

Kneeling beside the bed, he closes his eyes and opens his hands, with his palms facing upward. After praying aloud in Jamaican patois dialect, he goes and looks in the bathroom mirror. "Guess it's time to say goodbye." He pulls shears and clippers from the bag he'd laid on the counter the night before, takes a deep breath and cuts off his dreads—one by one. Thirty minutes later he's completely bald.

He stares at his image. "I'll keep facial hair. Nobody around here has seen me with a full beard, not even Gerald. The gray contacts help too." He steps in the shower and lets the warm water soothe his exhausted body. *I hate I had to leave Jacqueline, shouldn't have married her in the first place. Can't imagine the pain she's going through. What was I thinking, allowing my heart to go there again? That's the last time. At 48, I don't want to cause any woman any more suffering. Time to make amends.*

For the next couple of weeks Benjamin watches the Lamar family from afar, being careful to never get close enough that Gerald recognizes him. Given that the killer has already targeted Trey, he focuses most of his surveillance on him and Celeste. One night he follows Trey to a restaurant, then waits for him to be seated. Benjamin requests a table on the other side of the room that has a clear view of Trey.

As he watches Trey, he feels a sense of pride in his chiseled facial features and how mature he seems. The waiter comes to Benjamin's table and gives his spiel of what the special is for that day. He smiles and asks for more time to peruse the menu. Once the waiter leaves, Benjamin looks over at Trey's table and chokes on the water he's sipping.

His heartbeat races as he stares at the person who has joined Trey. The gray at her temples reminds him of how long it's been since he's seen her. She's thinner than he remembers. Her caramel skin is still flawless. The way she slightly leans her head to one side when she laughs, forces the memory of her scent to resurface from the crevices of his mind. Since marrying Jacqueline he's tried his best to keep those thoughts at bay. Now with her so close, yet so far, they come flooding back.

When she glances in his direction, he bows his head, puts his hat on, and throws a 20 dollar bill on the table. His mind reels as he rushes out of the restaurant and breaks all speed limits driving back to the hotel. After sitting on the side of the bed for a few minutes, and gulping down several straight shots of gin, Benjamin stretches out in the bed and closes his eyes. "Camilla."

Around midnight, Benjamin wakes up and realizes he's still fully dressed. His stomach growls. "I forgot to eat, shit." He orders room service and takes a shower while waiting on delivery. When the knock comes, he answers the door wearing a hotel towel from the waist down, and nothing else.

The 20something, blonde-haired, blue-eyed service attendant gives him a quick onceover, from his huge feet all the way up to his sleepy gray eyes. "Dayum! Oops, excuse me, sir." She sniggers and turns beet red. "Did you order room service?"

Benjamin looks down at her and smiles. "I sure did, beautiful one." He takes the tray, and asks her to hold on while he sits it down. She gladly holds the door open to see what he's working with from behind, fans herself and whispers, "Lord Jesus, thank you for making sure my shift ended with an eyeful of vanilla-chocolate candy."

He comes back to the door, takes the pen she offers and signs the tab. "Did you say something?"

"No, sir." She stares at him for a few more seconds. "Um, I'm sorry. I just have to tell you; you're one gorgeous man."

"One gorgeous *old* man." Benjamin chuckles. "But I appreciate the compliment. You have a good night."

As he closes the door, he spots a familiar face at the end of the hall. "That son-of-bitch."

Landis is grinding all up on some hooker-looking hood rat. Benjamin contains his urge to roll up on 'em and cold-cock his ass. Since Landis has no idea who he is—and at the moment isn't paying attention to anyone except that trick—Benjamin flips his doorstopper, grabs his cell phone off of the dresser, and casually snaps three pictures.

Chapter Ten

Tip buzzes his new admin-assistant. "Yolanda?"

"Yes, Mr. Collier, your next appointment is here: Mr. Josiah Norman and his grandson." She eyes the two men sitting across from her. "You ready for them?"

"I told you, whenever I buzz you, that means I'm available for my next appointment."

Yolanda looks up at the men. "Mr. Collier will see you now." She pulls her cell-phone out and sends Tip a text.

"He's Methuselah. Get thru quik, b4 he dies N ur office."

Tip reads it and smiles, then opens his office door and is taken aback by the gentleman rolling in on an electric wheelchair. He looks around 100 years old, has an oxygen tank strapped to the back of his chair, and the tube in his nose. His leathery skin was probably pecan-tan in younger years, but now is darkened in certain areas.

Even with all that, the man's back is straight, chin squared, and he wears a suit that's more expensive than the one Tip's sporting.

"Mr. Norman." Tip offers his hand to shake, and the elderly man obliges.

"Just 'Josiah', please. I'm not up for formalities," he says in a congested, nasally voice. He nods his head in the direction of the young man standing behind him."This is Amos, my grandson and primary caregiver."

Tip shakes Amos's hand and offers him a seat in the leather chair beside Josiah. "How about I call you 'Mr. Josiah' so my mama won't take a strap to me for not using a handle of respect," he says to the older man. "Most people call me 'Tip'."

Josiah laughs and wheezes all at once. "Sounds like a good, strong traditional mother. They're rare these days."

Tip answers, "Yes, sir. She always keeps me going. Couldn't ask for a better one." He sits behind his desk.

"How long have you been a private investigator?" Amos asks.

Tip loves answering this question. "Almost 30 years. Started at 22 and next month I'll be 52. I have a crew of 15 on staff here who are all more than competent because I trained them. How can I help you two gentlemen?"

The two men glance at one another, then back at Tip. Josiah finally answers. "Well, I'm hoping that we can be of assistance to one ano . . ." He starts a hacking cough that lasts longer than Tip is comfortable with.

Amos reaches into the small backpack hanging beside the oxygen tank, and hands Josiah an inhaler. Josiah takes a few puffs.

Tip buzzes Yolanda and asks her to bring a bottle of water.

"That ain't necessary, he'll be okay in a minute," Amos states, while rubbing Josiah's back.

Josiah breaths in deeply, slowly exhales and continues, "I'm an old man in horrible health, as I'm sure you've noticed. It's gotten to where my doctor says it's time for hospice care."

Tip leans forward and rests his hands flat on the desk. "I'm sorry to hear that."

"No need to be. I'm 86. As them old preachers say, 'we all got to go that way sooner or later," Josiah says. "I'm just not sure which way my cantankerous fossil of an ass is going." He doesn't wheeze when he laughs this time.

Amos tells Josiah, "I think we'd better state our business."

Josiah nods his head, then looks straight into Tip's eyes. "I was trying not to do this in a way that would upset you. My fighting days are long gone and . . . " He takes another puff of his inhaler. "I'm a man about peace, who wants to die in peace."

Tip gets an eerie feeling the longer he and Josiah eyeball one another. "Hold on, gentlemen." He picks up his receiver and buzzes Yolanda. "Can you come in here a minute?"

Yolanda knows something's wrong by the sound of Tip's voice. She quickly walks into his office, closes the door and stands there.

Tip opens the right-hand drawer of his desk. "Say what you came here to say," he tells Josiah.

Josiah notices Tip's eyes are now more green than blue. "I believe you've already figured it out, son."

"I ain't your son, old man." Tip replies, without blinking.

"No," Josiah answers, "but Shirley . . . was my daughter."

Chapter Eleven

Tip reaches into the drawer, then places his revolver on top of his desk. Yolanda swiftly walks over and stands beside him.

Amos stands up. "That's totally unnecessary."

Josiah reaches up and pats Amos's forearm, motioning for him to sit back down. "Just stay calm. There's no need for this to get out of hand."

Tip glances up at Amos. "Yeah 'Pretty Ricky', you need to listen to ya decrepit sugar-daddy. Put your high-yella ass back in that chair."

Amos reluctantly sits. "He's my grandfather."

Josiah chortles. "No sense in lying to the man, Amos. He's been a private detective longer than you've been alive, but that's neither here nor there. Now, Tip, please put your gun away. Those things make me nervous."

"That stays right where it is," Tip says. Yolanda puts her hand on Tip's shoulder. He turns and smiles at her. "I'm fine. Don't worry." He puts his gaze back on Josiah. "Your *Tales of the Crypt* ass better get to explaining why the fuck you're trying to kill off my family."

"What? He never done nothing to your family." Amos shouts. "All he wanted was a chance to help his grandson." He claps his hands to emphasize each word.

"Did I pull your chain, motherfucker?" Tip asks Amos, while still staring at Josiah. "And both of you better keep my son's name out ya mouth. You rolled up in here with an agenda. Depending on what it is, you might roll out of here on a gurney."

Yolanda finally speaks. "Everybody just calm the hell down, please. Just bring it down." She raises both hands and points her index fingers towards the floor. "Don't nobody need to die up in here today."

Josiah shakes his head and frowns at Tip. "I agree with this lovely young lady. If you'll give me a chance to tell my side of the story, I know you'll see things differently."

"Your side better include why you killed a woman I loved like a daughter."

Josiah's hands shake. "I have no idea what you're talking about. I'd never do that. I'm a retired Vietnam vet and successful businessman, and have lived my whole life helping others."

"Did you know Calvin Wells?"

"Yes, I hired him when you moved here. Just wanted to keep my promise to Shirley and watch over her son."

Tip furrows his brows. "That's a crock of bullshit. If you were that concerned why didn't you contact me from the get-go, instead of putting some sleaze-ball in my child's life?"

"Shirley forbade me talking to you. You know she was mentally ill. I was afraid if I called you she'd stop communicating with me. I loved my girl." Josiah wipes his eyes and mouth with a handkerchief. "You don't understand."

"I'm listening," Tips says.

Josiah rests his hands in his lap and closes his eyes. "In 1957 I was on leave and stationed in Atlanta. One night a tall, slender college girl—who was dark as night and a dream to behold—showed up in the club me and my buddies frequented."

"Shelia Lamar," Tip states, referring to Gerald's mother and finally realizing he knows one side of this saga.

"Yes, we both drank too much that night and . . . things happened. When I got up the next morning she was gone. I spent the last two weeks of my leave looking for her, and came up empty handed. When I was on leave again a year later, I searched every college in the University Center again and finally ran into the friend who was with her the night we met.

"She told me everything. You know, some women can't hold water. I found out Sherman and Mary Ann Douglas had adopted Shirley, and located their address, but was afraid to reveal who I was. I sat parked across from their home for days, and watched them come and go . . . with my only child.

"For the next 18 years, I sent a money-order equaling almost every dime of my paycheck to their house. Never missed a month. After her adoptive parents both passed, and she went off to college, I had no idea where she'd moved to.

"It took so long for me to find her again after all those years. I was heartbroken to find out she was in prison, and wrote her a letter introducing myself. When she wrote back and asked to meet in person, I was so happy. Started visiting her at least twice a month." Josiah begins weeping and dabs his eyes with his handkerchief.

Amos gets up, stands behind him and massages his shoulders. He gives Tip a somber look. "He hasn't slept through the night one time since he found out Shirley died. The liaison officer never told him she was sick or in the hospital. Just answered his call one day and reported she was gone."

Josiah gathers himself. "I'll do whatever is necessary to make you see the only thing I'm guilty of is loving my daughter. Harming your family is out of the question. After what I went through in Nam, I'd never think of killing anyone, never in a million years." He groans. "My only agenda today is begging you for a chance to meet my grandson before I die."

Chapter Twelve

October rolls around and Gerald's family seems to be back to normal. The relief of knowing Wells is dead brings a peace he hadn't felt in months.

Tip held no grudges against Josiah once he agreed to police interrogation, and their determination was he had nothing to do with Sonya's death. Before Josiah and Amos left Dallas, Tip had taken his son over to their hotel to meet Josiah, and the elderly gentleman cried a river.

There is something inside Tip that still doesn't feel right. "All this played out too easily," he tells Gerald, as they share beers in Gerald's den.

"Yeah, I felt that way for awhile, but all is still quiet. I think it's about time we exhale and get back to enjoying life." Gerald sips his Heineken. "Trey's doing a whole lot better. One good thing about all of this is he's sharing a close bond with Camilla again. Just pray Celeste gets there too."

Bridget walks in, hands Gerald another beer, and takes the empty bottle. She sticks her tongue out at Tip. "You don't get another one, had too much at your party. I betcha can't even stand up."

"Woman, you ain't got to give me a damn thing," Tips says, reaching into his pocket. "I'm like the Boy Scouts." He raises a flask filled with V.S.O.P. "Always prepared." They all laugh.

"See, that's why you'll be crashing here tonight." Bridget kisses Tip on the cheek. "Happy birthday, with ya old ass. You need a wife."

"What I tell you about saying that four letter word to me? I got plenty of company—giving me plenty, then I gets my ass up and goes home."

Bridget throws Tip a 'talk-to-the-hand' jester, climbs onto Gerald's lap and wraps her arms around his neck. "Baby, I'm really worried about Celeste. Did you see how she was acting today, her face hanging to the floor?"

"Yeah, and Landis is missing from family gatherings more than not lately. You should talk to her, sweetheart."

"I tried today," Bridget says, "but she may as well not have been here for the little interaction she had with us. I'm glad she left Lia here. Maybe a couple of days alone with Landis will help." She leans forward and looks over at Tip. "Is that fool snoring?" Bridget bursts out laughing.

Gerald joins her. "Guess I'd better help him to his bedroom."

Celeste pulls up to the valet at the hotel and dials Landis' number as she gives the attendant her keys. When voicemail comes on she hangs up and speed-dials 10.

"Good evening, Celeste, are you there?" Walt asks.

"Yes. Is he?" She walks toward the lobby.

"He checked in around three, and they left about two hours ago. I followed them to a restaurant off of Bachman Lake. They're about 15 minutes away now. Do I need to stick around?"

"I got this, Walter. Thanks for your help." She strolls up to one of the front desk clerks and flashes a big smile. "Hi, my husband already checked in today, and said he left a key for me. Would you be a darling and get it. He won't be back for an hour or so, and I must get in that Jacuzzi tub. This has been a rather long day."

"Sure," The clerks says. "What's the name and room number?"

"Mr. and Mrs. Landis Faber. Room 20172."

The clerk types into her computer. "You're right; there it is. May I see your license for identification?"

Celeste puts her license on the desk.

The clerk looks at it and hands it back to her. "Hold on one moment and I'll get that extra key."

When she enters the huge suite, she rolls her eyes and pours herself a drink, then sits in the chair in front of the bar. A few minutes later the door opens, and Landis comes in with his tongue all down some woman's throat, feeling her up. The woman starts unbuttoning his shirt. She shrieks when Celeste slams her glass down on the table.

Landis turns around, almost leaps to the other side of the room and reaches his hands out toward Celeste. "Baby, wait, wait now, don't. You, you don't want to do that!"

Celeste points a Glock straight at him. She pulls the magazine out of her purse and loads it.

The other woman screams, "Oh, shit, shit, Landis, I ain't down with this bullshit." She squirms like she's about to pee on herself.

"Shonda, shut up," Landis yells. "Celeste, baby, just put the gun down," he pleads. "You know you don't wanna hurt anybody." He pounds his chest. "You got me, okay, you got me. We need to talk about this."

"You need to tell ya bitch to leave before I blow her and that door the fuck up," Celeste commands, in a voice tone much too calm for Landis.

"Lady with the 9-mil, you ain't got to tell me twice. Ain't no man worth this." Shonda swings the door wide open and rushes out.

"You know what you've done to me?" Celeste still speaks no louder than her normal volume. "I told you when we got married not to ever bring your past indiscretions up in our home, and then after four years, you . . . I find out you been all up in some man. That was a man, Landis. What the fuck? Are you gay!"

Landis gets on his knees. "Baby, please, let's just sit down and talk. I didn't want it to end like this."

She cocks her head to the side. "Oh, so how the hell did you see this ending? Did 'cleaving only unto you until death do us part' mean anything to you?"

"It means everything to me."

"Shut up, just shut up. Shut the hell up. Get up off your damn knees."

Someone bangs on the door. "Hotel security, ma'am. Is everything all right in there?"

Landis and Celeste stare at one another for about five minutes. He blows her a kiss and mouths the words "forgive me."

Celeste holds back tears as she pops the magazine out. She puts it and her gun back in her purse, then goes and opens the door.

The security guard asks again if everything's all right and she responds in a deflated tone, "You know, I thought it was but . . . it never was, and won't be for a long time." She brushes past him and slowly walks toward the elevator, with Landis shouting her name in the background.

Benjamin opens his door enough to see Celeste make the turn down the hall. When he hears the elevator doors shut, he walks down to Landis' room and knocks.

Landis opens the door with a frustrated look on his face, holding a full shot-glass. Before he can say anything Benjamin grabs him by the collar, shoves him inside and slams him up against the door.

"Don't ever say another got-damn word to her," he says, through clinched teeth. "Don't go near her again. You hear me?"

"Man, who the fuck are you, and why you telling me what I can and can't do with my wi—"

Benjamin hurls Landis to the floor and gives him a punch in the face so hard it knocks him unconscious, and then slips back out of the room.

Chapter Thirteen

Celeste puts her car in reverse. Landis drives up and blocks her. She reaches into her briefcase, then gets out. "I know damn well you didn't bring your ass over here this morning. Get out of my way."

Landis charges in her direction yelling, "You think you're going to get away from me, trying to scare me with some O.G.?"

"What the hell are you talking about?" Celeste keeps her arms to her side.

"I'm talking 'bout that hood who almost killed me right after you left." He rushes up closer to her. "You see these stitches in my chin? He bum-rushed and hit me so hard I was out for over 30 minutes."

"First of all, I didn't sick nobody on you. Secondly, come any closer and I'll finish what I started yesterday. Now get out of my way so I can go to work. What we had is over and you're the cause of it, nobody else."

Their neighbor across the street peeks out of her window.

"Please, just leave," Celeste says. You're making a scene." She tries to open her car door but Landis slams it shut, and gets up in her face.

"That's all you ever care about, you and your crazy ass family. Always concerned about how things look to everybody else. I've felt like I was in a fishbowl since the day we started dating."

Tears well in Celeste's eyes as they stare at one another. "There it is. Yep, I knew it was coming. So, you screwing men is my fault now, my family's fault?"

Landis lowers his gaze.

"That's what I thought. Why did you even marry me, to put on a front? Didn't want the world to know you, an ex pro basketball player, are gay? Tell me what the point was."

"I'm not gay, I'm bisexual," Landis whispers. "If I had told you that when we first met, you wouldn't have given me the time of day. This is who I truly am, baby. Can we go inside and talk, without all the anger?" He touches her face and she slaps his hand away.

"Move right now, or I'll ram your precious Porsche so hard it can't be repaired. Gay, or straight or bi, you're nothing but a sorry, lying, cheating piece of shit."

Landis grabs her by the neck and slams her body up on the hood of her car. "You not leaving me, not ever. I got too much invested in this, bitch."

The neighbor runs out of her house. "Stop, that. You leave her alone. I called the police and they're on their way. You get your hands off her!"

All of a sudden Landis' head jerks back and he falls to the ground.

A couple of hours later Gerald, Bridget and Tip are met at the police station by Chief Jack Shaw. He shakes Gerald and Bridget's hands, then greets Tip. "Collier," he says, in a no-love-lost-between-us tone.

"Shaw," Tip responds, in a tone that says he agrees.

"Where's Celeste?" Gerald asks. "What happened? Is my baby all right?"

"Mrs. Faber is in my office. When we got to her residence, Mr. Faber was lying in a pool of blood, and she was standing over him, in a trance like state. The ambulance got there in time to resuscitate him, but we haven't been able to get anything out of her. Your son's already here. Please follow me."

When they get in the office Celeste gets up, reaches out, holds on to her father's neck, and weeps.

Gerald takes a seat next to her and holds her in his arms. "Sweetie, what happened?" He rubs her arms. "Chief told me Landis is fighting for his life? Come on now, you've got to stop crying, okay? Give your statement to Shaw and we'll move forward with whatever needs to be done."

Trey interposes, "She wanted to wait for you to get here."

Celeste prays, "Please, Lord, help me," under her breath, then turns to face the chief. "I'm ready."

Chief Shaw hits the record button.

She details everything that happened beginning with the evening before, up to the time Landis grabs her neck. "I was so shocked he would hurt me. He's never been abusive. It's like he became a whole other person." She wipes her eyes with the handkerchief Bridget gives her.

"All I had in my hand was a taser." Her voice cracks. "I never ever intended to use it, nor the gun the night before."

Gerald rubs her back. "Take your time and tell us what else happened."

"That's what I'm still not clear on," she explains. "When he was choking me I closed my eyes and . . . the next thing I know he grunts, I look up into his eyes and he falls to the ground." She exhales a big breath of air. "After that Mrs. Gantz is screaming from across the street, and Landis lying there with a bullet in the side of his neck." She covers her face with her shaky hands. "The doctors say the bullet hit his spinal cord; if he makes it, he's likely to be paralyzed the rest of his life. He's had one surgery and will have another one in a couple of days, if he lives."

Trey asks, "Chief Shaw, did you find anything in her home or car to connect her to this shooting?"

The chief leans forward. "No, she only had one firearm, the 9 millimeter in her purse. The ammunition doesn't match the one medical personnel found in his spinal cord. It was a .308 shot from a modified Winchester, and whoever shot him, was proficient. We searched the area and got statements from neighbors, but most of them were at work when the shooting occurred. Mrs. Gantz was most helpful because she witnessed the whole event, but still didn't see who shot him."

"So they were aiming at him and not Celeste?" Gerald asks, with an anxious look on his face.

"Most definitely," Chief Shaw answers. "A pro like that, doesn't make that big of a mistake. They were definitely after your son-in-law."

Bridget puts her hand over her mouth. "Lord, have mercy."

"Mrs. Faber, do you have any idea who the man was your husband told you about that attacked him?" Chief Shaw asks.

Trey speaks up. "If she did she would have told you. All she had to do was keep that part of the story out if she was hiding something; she didn't." He stands and takes Celeste by the hand. "If there's nothing more, we're leaving."

Celeste's tears stop and attorney mode kicks in, once the chief asks her that question."Trey's right. I've cooperated fully with this investigation, and will continue to do so. No more questions will be answered today though. I have to go home and try to explain all this to our daughter."

Benjamin drives to Carrolton, TX. After dismantling the rifle, he ditches its parts into three different dumpsters, blocks apart from one another. By the time he gets back to Dallas, every news station in Texas has the incident highlighted in headlines. He watches the film of paparazzi swooping down on Gerald and his family as they leave the police station.

Benjamin sits on the sofa and takes a couple of sips from his gin and orange juice. "I had to do it, baby girl. He was hurting you. That's not what I came there to do, but what other choice did I have? I told that mofo not to come near you again, and he turns around and puts his hands on you? Was I supposed to sit there and let him kill you? His bitch ass was warned; he should have heeded."

Chapter Fourteen

Later that night the whole family gathers in the living room at Gerald and Bridget's home. Celeste holds Lia to her bosom, and begins singing her favorite hymn: *Even Me.* Bridget joins in with her rich lower register, and the lovely harmony rings through the house.

When Lia falls asleep, Marcus offers to take her and Little Tip upstairs to their bedrooms. He kisses Bridget on the cheek as he leaves. "This sure ain't how I planned on starting my last year of high school, Ma."

"When you get them settled, son, come on back downstairs. It's time we stopped leaving you out of our discussions. You're an adult now," Gerald tells him.

"Yes, sir."

Tip moves closer to Celeste on the couch, and she lays her head on his chest. He kisses her forehead. The room is silent until Marcus returns.

"Before you sit down, Marcus, I would like to do something I've been neglectful in over the past few months—family prayer. Trey, I know you're not a religious person, but if you would, please join us." Gerald gets choked up. "My children are suffering and I feel the best I have to offer right now is what I believe."

Bridget stands, hugs him and grabs his hand, then reaches the other one out to Trey. When everyone is finally in the circle, Gerald prays. Celeste begins to weep again. When the prayer is finished, Trey walks over, grabs and holds her in his arms. Marcus brushes away tears as he wraps his arms around both of them.

The next day Celeste puts her house on the market, and temporarily moves in with Trey. Although her maid has cleaned all the blood stains from her driveway, she still can't bring herself to go home. "Thank goodness the house is only in my name," she tells her realtor, and asks her to look for a home in Trey's neighborhood.

After a couple of weeks, Landis begins breathing on his own and regains full consciousness. Celeste's feels relieved and starts bringing Lia to the hospital two or three times a week. She and Landis never say much more than hello to one another. He avoids looking at her most of the time. One day when she visits without Lia, his mother verbally assaults her before she gets in the room good.

"You did this, you nasty whore. Landis told me all about your wandering ways. You ought to be ashamed of yourself, going around screwing all over the city. And why would you hire a hit man to kill my baby?" She hisses. "He's gonna be paralyzed from the neck down for the rest of his life. Stay away from him!"

Celeste looks at her like she's got two heads. "Gladys, you need to step your loony ass the hell back. I didn't do a thing to your son except love him, and that wasn't enough." She walks over and stares at Landis.

He turns his head to the opposite wall. "I have nothing to say to you, bitch."

"How the hell do you come out of a near death experience and still stoop even lower?" Celeste slaps his face. "Look at me, damn it; you owe me at least that much. Tell Gladys the truth or I'll tell her, and every news outlet in this country. You lived a lie the whole four years we were married, not me!"

Gladys pulls on Celeste's arm. "Take your hands off my boy; he's done with you. I'm taking him home with me when he gets out of here."

Celeste jerks her arm away from Gladys clutches. "Old heifer, if you don't get your foolish ass out of my face. You can have your 'boy', but while you're busy nursing him on ya droopy titties, ask him why I found him in a hotel room with his tongue almost touching another man's tonsils, while feeling all up and down his penis."

Gladys' mouth falls open, as Celeste storms toward the door, then turns around. "Landis, I hope you and your mother will be a happy couple, yet I doubt it 'cause she's not your type. I'll send you divorce papers as soon as you're discharged."

When she gets in her car she calls Bridget.

"Celeste, are you okay?"

"I need to clear my head," Celeste responds, speaking barely above a whisper. "You know, get away for a little while, change of atmosphere."

"Well you know we'll keep the baby. That's never a problem."

"No, she . . . I need her there too, and was wondering if you'd go with us up to the cabin in Sulfur, maybe the week after next. Mama's coming to visit Trey and I'm totally in no mood for her." Celeste starts her car and turns on the air conditioner.

"That's a good idea. I'll be glad to go."

"Thank you so much. I have to set my clients up to call Trey if they need anything. He's always got my back, but I wanna make sure I leave things at the firm as tight as possible."

Celeste doesn't say goodbye, nor hang up. After a few moments of silence, Bridget calls her name.

"Yes, ma'am," Celeste answers.

"Those tears are normal, but don't you beat up on yourself. You did nothing wrong. Don't let Landis guilt trip you. Remember you're talking to somebody who knows way too much about that pain, girl. I loved your uncle so much I thought I would die. Started looking in the mirror every day, wondering stupid stuff like was I small enough, pretty enough; did he want someone with longer hair and lighter complexion? All my insecurities were haunting me."

Celeste sniffles. "I'm still in a state of shock. Landis was my whole world. How could he?" She cries, and leans her head up against the car window. "How did you survive that, Auntie?"

Bridget smiles. "God, and your father." She shakes her head. "Gerald called me one night out of the blue. That's when he finally revealed why he gave me 'Jet' for a nickname. Told me I was a beautiful black queen. Your father is a man of few words, but the words he does say, are the ones that matter. You keep your head up. I'm a witness, this too shall pass, understand?"

"Dad doesn't want us talking about this, but I'm so sorry you went through all that."

Bridget exhales. "*We* went through through that, but it's all in the past. I've forgiven them, and my life is right where it should be now. You'll get there. I pray someday so does your father. Call me next week and let me know when we're leaving for our mini-vacation."

"Yes, ma'am, I will, and I love you."

"I love you too. Go home and get some rest."

Chapter Fifteen

Gerald's body jerks and he balls up his fists. "No, no!" he yells, then tosses and turns while his body jerks, flailing his arms so much Bridget gets out of bed. His shouts get louder. "Stop this shit. You, you can't have 'em; leave us alone. I'm gonna kill your ass!"

Bridget goes to the bathroom, comes back with a cold damp face towel and sits on his side of the bed. "Gerald, honey, wake up. Gerald?"

His eyes pop open. "What!" When he sees Bridget he relaxes and sighs heavily. "Oh, Lord, I did it again?"

"Yes," she answers. "It's been awhile since you've had one this bad. Take some deep breaths, so your heart rate will calm." She uses the towel to wipe sweat from his face and upper-body.

Gerald sits up, and pulls her into his arms. "Did I hurt you like last time, did I?" He examines her face closely. "Baby, I would never, ever put my hands on you in anger, you know that."

Bridget smiles. "Look here, gentle giant, I'm fine. I got out of bed when you started, and sweetheart, that was only one time." She taps his nose with her finger.

He strokes a stray loc of hair from her eyes. "One time is too many. I'll remember that bruise on your face forever." He hugs her and whispers in her ear, "Why do you put up with me and all my damn dysfunctions? I feel like a such rotten husband sometimes."

Bridget gently pushes him back so they are looking in one another's face. He tries to lower his head, but she puts her finger under his chin and lifts it. "We are one, been one for over four years. I ain't going nowhere, no matter how hard you try to run me off." She laughs.

Gerald's face is still solemn. "I love you more than you'll ever know."

"Enough to face those nightmares?"

He runs his fingers through her hair, starts unbuttoning her top and kissing where each button was.

After a few minutes of that, Bridget begins purring. "You always do this to get off this subject."

"And it works too, right?" He looks into her eyes, then eases his head down and starts biting her breast gently.

She moans. "Um . . . someday it won't, but . . ."

He sucks her nipple.

"Woo, it's working tonight." Bridget throws the towel onto the floor, pushes Gerald back down in the bed, and climbs on top of him.

Benjamin watches as Walter pulls up to Trey's house and helps Celeste load up what looks like a week's worth of luggage. He is far enough away that binoculars are needed to get a close view of them. Since arriving a month and a half ago he had traded days watching either Trey's or Celeste's comings and goings. Now that she's moved in with Trey, he can watch over both of them at the same time.

The family seems satisfied that they're no longer in danger, but Benjamin's skepticism is still high. "They think Wells planted that bomb, but I know better. I saw that old man with Tip, so I know he wouldn't trust him if he was shady. Somebody's still a threat."

After Celeste fastens Lia into her car seat and gets in the passenger seat, Walter slides in on the driver's side. Benjamin decides not to follow them since Walter is their escort. He's done a thorough background check on Walter and knows he's a stand-up guy and close family friend.

About an hour later a limo pulls into Trey's driveway. The chauffeur opens the door and Benjamin is rendered speechless once again. Camilla gets out wearing a formfitting red dress and high-heels. It takes every ounce of his willpower not to drive up, grab and throw her in the car and drive off into 'happily ever after'. "Come on, man, get a grip. Stay focused. That isn't water under the bridge; it washed the bridge out. You're here to help Gerald keep the family safe." He leans his head back against the headrest and closes his eyes. *You're engraved in my heart and I still love you; it's just that I know now—blood comes first.*

Celeste hands Lia a small bag and tells her to put it in the far bedroom of the cabin. Lia struts off, proud to be helping like a big girl.

"I'm so glad we did this. That ride was therapeutic, and this cool, fresh Oklahoma air feels wonderful," Celeste says.

"It sure does." Bridget pulls off her hat and puts it on the table. "I got me a good nap in the car too, and . . ."

Lia suddenly lets out a piercing scream. Walt and Celeste sprint to the back room, with Bridget right on their trail. When they get to Lia she's pointing at the walls. "Miss Sonya, Miss Sonya. Mommy, that's Miss Sonya!"

Walt picks Lia up and passes her to Bridget. Celeste stands as stiff as a statue and stares at the walls; walls that have Sonya's picture plastered on almost every spot. There are sticky notes, and notebook paper with writing on them tacked to each photo. Handwriting that's all too familiar to Celeste.

"I'm taking the baby up front. Walter, please call the police," Bridget says frantically.

"No!" Celeste speaks without looking in Bridget's direction. "Not yet, please, no police yet." She walks in a circle and tries to take it all in. "Oh my God. Ooh my God." Her breathing gets arduous so she sits on the bed.

Walter pulls out his cell-phone and dials a number. He gets an answer after the first ring.

"Collier and Associates, this is Yolanda speaking."

Chapter Sixteen

Around an hour and a half later Tip and Gerald peruse the premises escorted by Murray County Oklahoma Sherriff's deputies.

One of the deputies chats with Chief Shaw via cell-phone, giving him an update. "Yes, sir, looks like we've got a classic stalking case gone bad here. There's several, what looks like, attempted bomb creations and tons of ammunition in there. This is one sick perp."

Celeste still sits on the edge of the bed in the room that's practically wallpapered with Sonya's images. Wearing synthetic gloves, she stares at a note in her trembling hands, and reads it aloud for the third time. This time with her brother listening.

"Dear Sonya,

You rejected me on every turn, yet fell for a man who throws his ratchet ass thots up in your face like it's no big deal? I could've loved you so much better than that. Why did you throw yourself

at him?

I'm heartbroken. I have to do this, can't you see that? If I can't

have you, nobody will, nobody!

You're forever mine,

Landis"

Trey bangs out of the cabin door, almost ripping it off its hinges, and heads to the driver's side of Walt's SUV. "Give me the keys," He demands, with fury in his eyes.

"You know I'm not gonna do that," Walter answers, in a calm but stern voice.

Trey marches up to his best friend and stands toe to toe with him. "Walt, give me the got-damn keys!" he barks.

Walt doesn't move. "Man, I'm not gonna let you ruin your life over this. You gotta let the law handle it. If you drive back to Dallas and go to that hospital like this, you'll be in jail tonight. I'm not about to let that happen and you know this."

"Did you forget who works for whom. You better get your big ass out my way," Trey yells, and takes a swing at Walter.

Walter leans away from the punch and puts Trey in an arm wrench hold so tight he can't move. "Now, I'm gonna act like you didn't say that to me due to your frame of mind right now. Settle your ass down, or I'll hold you like this until it's time to leave. We can't be showing out in front of the law. You got too much to lose to be going out like that. You know I'm right."

Trey takes a few deep breaths, knowing his friend means business. "Okay, let me go," he says in a soother voice tone. "He killed her; his bitch ass killed my baby!" After he rants a few more minutes, he hangs his head and fights back tears. "I'm good. Get off me. I'm good."

Walt releases the hold and Trey starts jogging down the road, punching air. Walt follows him.

By the time Gerald and family gets back to Dallas, Landis has been put under arrest for the murder of Sonya, and making a terrorist threat toward Trey. The Dallas County Sherriff's department has 2 deputies on guard around the clock at his hospital door; only his attorney is allowed to visit.

An initial hearing is set for a month later, when doctor's foresee he'll be physically well enough to be discharged.

News reporters hound Celeste to the point she shuts down on everyone. Bridget keeps Lia with her to give Celeste time to rest her mind and heal as much as possible.

Needing a distraction from all the madness, Trey tries to keep working, but gets very little done.

Benjamin remains in Dallas, determined to be there at least until the trial is over. He rents a townhouse and allows himself to relax a little.

Reporters swarm the courthouse stairs like mosquitoes the day of the hearing. The whole Lamar family is in the courtroom. When he's wheeled in, Landis avoids looking in their direction. Trey and Celeste hold one another's hands tightly when the judge asks, "In the case of the State of Texas versus Mr. Landis Omari Faber, for murder and threat of terror, how does the defendant plead?"

Landis stares down at his knees when his attorney responds, "Not guilty by reason of temporary insanity, Your Honor."

People moan all over the courtroom.

Celeste buries her head in Trey's shoulder. He turns and kisses her on the cheek. "That motherfucker, I knew he'd do that," he hisses.

After the judge bangs her gavel a few times to restore order, Landis' attorney requests the judge put him on house arrest given that his poor health removes the threat of him fleeing. The state's attorney argues that he's still a danger to society, yet the judge grants the request. She stipulates that Landis' home be heavily guarded, and only his attorney, and home health nurses allowed interaction with him.

The trial is set to begin on December 12th.

"He'd better hope he lives that long," Benjamin says under his breath, from his seat in the far back.

Chapter Seventeen

Bridget stamps up the staircase in Trey's house, enters Celeste's bedroom and pulls the drapes all the way open. When the sunlight streams in Celeste opens her eyes wide. "What the hell?"

"Celeste Cecelia, get your ass out of this bed right now!" Bridget walks over and pulls all the cover off the bed. "It's Thanksgivings Day, and I'll be damn if you're gonna lie in this bed, in the doggone dark for one more minute. You've been this way for the most part of five weeks."

Celeste puts her arm over her eyes. "I'm not in the mood for this. Ain't no way I'm gonna pretend to be thankful for the bullshit that's going on in my life. Y'all go on with the charade; I'm no longer interested in participating. Please put my covers back on the bed."

Bridget climbs in bed from the other side. "Oh, yeah, well aren't you forgetting somebody, the greatest blessing in your life?"

Celeste doesn't move.

Bridget turns on her phone and plays a video. Lia sweet voice fills the room.

"Mommy, when is you comin' to get me. Big Pa keep sayin' it but you haven't come. You don't want me no more?" She starts weeping. *"Mommy please, come get me. I don't know where my daddy is."*

Celeste sits up with tears streaming, and Bridget hands her the phone. "Neither of you have called her in over two weeks. Do you realize what y'all doing to your child?" She pulls Celeste into her arms, holds and rocks her. "You have the best little girl in the world to be thankful for. It's time to get up and go on, baby. Lia needs you."

"That's enough talk." Gerald comes in and lifts Celeste off the bed, cradles her in his arms and takes her into the bathroom. After he sits her down on the commode, he kneels on one knee and looks her dead in her eyes. "Pumpkin, you get in the shower or I'm going to put you there, pajamas and all. You hear me? I'm giving you 30 minutes to get clean, dressed and downstairs in the limo. Tonight when you leave our house, Lia is coming back here with you.

"No matter what was going on in my life when you were children, I never neglected y'all—not ever. This shit ends right now. Stop putting Landis before Lia. Nobody is as important to you as she, especially not his sorry ass." He stands. "We'll be waiting downstairs." He exits with Bridget behind him.

That evening at dinner Lia clings to Celeste until she falls asleep in her arms. Claudette takes her from Celeste and heads upstairs to lay her down. Little Tip is on her heels, rubbing his eyes.

Celeste pours her fifth glass of wine, but Trey intercepts it before she picks it up."Sis, you need to slow down on that."

Celeste takes a swig straight from the bottle and bangs it back down on the table. "I'm celebrating Thanksgivings. That's what we're here for, right, dad? It's a celebration." She stares at Gerald.

"Trey, get that from her," Gerald orders, staring back at Celeste. "You need to go lie down with your daughter and sleep it off."

"I think that's a good idea," Tip says.

Celeste swerves her neck around and looks at him. "Shit, I know you not lecturing me on liquor, as many bottles I done seen you turn up." She laughs. "Don't even trip, man."

"Okay, that's enough," Gerald's bass voice echoes through their dining room. "You watch what you say; tipsy or not, don't ever disrespect Tip again. I know you're going through a tough time, but disrespect is not condoned under my roof. That hasn't changed. Now go lay your butt down and sober up."

"Or what? You gonna take your belt off and wallop me?" she snorts out loud and giggles.

Bridget stands up. "This dinner's over," she declares, "and there's no way I'm letting you take that baby home tonight acting a fool like this." She and Gerald have given the staff the holiday off so she starts clearing the table.

Celeste takes a drink from the wine bottle again and glares up at Bridget. "You know what, Auntie? You're not really my aunt." She points at Tip. "He's not really my uncle. Y'all 'bout as blood-kin to me and Trey as Marcus." She gazes at Gerald, who is still staring her down, with an annoyed look on his face. "And you . . ."

"Celeste, stop this bullshit, right now," Trey shouts. "You're not the only one at this table in pain. Your hurt is no more agonizing than mine, and doing this won't erase it." He reaches for the bottle, and Celeste jerks it back, sips and sits it back down again, without taking her eyes off Gerald.

Gerald stands. "You better not open your mouth to say what I think you're about to."

Celeste glares at him with a smirk. "You're not my father."

The sting of Bridget's slap cuts Celeste's next breath short. "Don't you ever say that to him again!" She snatches the bottle out of Celeste's hands and throws it to the floor so hard it smashes. "Since the day you were born"—she points in Celeste's face with one hand, and at Gerald with the other—"that man right there has loved, worked, wept, cussed over you two, and without so much as a 'thank you' in return. He is your daddy. There's more to being a father than donating sperm. Your drunk ass needs to go home and stop acting like a spoiled child. You're way too old for this. If he isn't your dad, who is?" She cuts her eyes at Celeste. "Say it. I dare you to to say it, so I can slap the snot out your nose again."

Gerald sits back down. "Ramon."

Every person in the room turns and looks at him, stunned.

"Yes, I said his name."

"Dad, you don't have to do this," Trey pleads. "She's just drunk. Don't put yourself through this. I'll take her home."

Gerald leans his elbows on the table and puts his large hands together in prayer position. "No, everybody, stay where you are. Bridget, baby, sit down, please." He still stares at his daughter.

"Yes, your father is Ramon. When we found that out, you and Trey promised me that meant nothing to you, that biology didn't trump all the years I put in raising you. So I put this unspoken rule in place that he was dead to me in every way and wouldn't even speak his name . . . until now." He leans back and folds his arms.

"But denying he ever existed, and requiring you all to do the same was foolish. Ramon has been gone what, over 9 years? I'm right where you are, pumpkin. At least you acknowledge your pain. Me, I got busy trying to fix it for all of us, but never letting God fix me. I have nightmares about him; it's been happening since I found out about him and Camilla. Had one so rough a couple months ago I

107

accidently hit Bridget and bruised her cheek." He shakes his head and closes his eyes. "My main heartache is from being betrayed by Ramon, not Camilla, but my brother. I've lived for all these years with anger so deep, I can't even verbalize it. Not even now."

After moments of silence, Celeste gets up, walks over to Gerald, hugs him and whispers, "I'm sorry." She glances at Tip. "Uncle Tip, please forgive me. I love you so much. You know?"

"That's all right, little girl," Tips says with a smile on his face. He winks at her. "But don't let it happen again or I'll make you cut a switch." Everyone laughs, removing some of the tension from the room.

Gerald pulls Celeste around and she snuggles up against his neck. He plants a kiss on her forehead. Trey calls his limo driver, and Bridget continues clearing the table.

"Ma, I'll get the mini-vac and clean up the glass," Marcus says softly.

"That would help a lot, dear," Bridget responds. "Thanks so much."

Benjamin stares out of his huge bay window. *I can't even eat dinner with my family.* The loneliness finally creeps in, as his frustration grows over not being able to come from out of the shadows. Being in close proximity, yet unable to reach out to Gerald, has become agitating; however, he knows it's for the best.

The vow of abstinence I took when I returned to Dallas is getting more and more difficult to endure. Damn, seeing Camilla so often makes it that much harder—literally. Every time I close my eyes, her face appears.

Chapter Eighteen

Celeste closes on a house around the corner from Trey and hurriedly moves in because Landis' trial date inches closer; she wants to be able to unwind in her own place after each court episode. She forces herself to return to work as a way to stop the pressure-cooker in her head from exploding.

At the beginning of December the *'ex famous pro basketball player turned stalker/murderer'* news stories are highlighted again. Trying not to let it pull her into a black hole, she agrees to go to a basketball game one evening with Marcus and Trey.

The next afternoon Trey gets a call from Gerald.

"Hey, man, ya'll must've had a great time last night. Marcus made up some excuse to not go to school today." They both chuckle.

"Yeah, it was pretty good. Celeste was acting like her old self again all night. I was happy to see that."

"Have you seen her today? She told us she was going to come get Lia this morning and spend the day working on cases from home, but we haven't heard from her. She's not answering our calls either."

"Come on, it's one o'clock. Sis is probably not even out of bed yet after the night we had. I'll have Walt run by there, all right?"

"Okay, I'm sure it's nothing, but you know how I am about ya'll," Gerald replies.

"I got you, dad. No worries."

Walter rings the doorbell to Celeste's house, then knocks hard when she doesn't answer. After the fourth knock he turns the doorknob and the door opens. "I done told that woman about not locking her door. Ain't never seen a more hardheaded person in my life." He shakes his head as he walks in shouting her name.

When she doesn't answer he climbs the stairs to the second story and searches to no avail. She isn't on the first story either when he checks all the rooms. "Probably in the basement, listening to her old school jams." He opens the door on the far end of her kitchen, jogs down the steps and sees her lying on the couch.

"Celeste, hey crazy. I told you about being by yourself with the door unlocked, and you got them headphones on." He moves closer to her as he speaks. "Woman, I know you hear . . . oh fuck!" Celeste's lips are blue; there's an empty pill bottle and empty half a pint of gin on the coffee table in front of her.

"Damn it! Don't you do this, Celeste." He calls 911 and tells them where to send the ambulance, then puts her on the floor and begins chest compressions. After the first round, he checks for a heartbeat and still finds none. Walt gives another set of rounds before the EMS and two police cars show up. He tells them he has no idea how long she's been like that.

The EMS gives Celeste a quick, thorough examination, then looks solemnly at Walt.

"No, don't." he falls back on his knees, pulls Celeste's body up and wraps her in his arms. "Please don't tell me it's too late, please."

"Sir, I'm sorry, we estimate she expired approximately 6-10 hours ago. Looks like she overdosed on *Anafranil* and alcohol."

One of the officers asks, "Are you her husband?"

Walter closes his eyes, shakes his head no, and continues to rock Celeste's body back and forth. "Aw . . . Celeste, why would you do this? You didn't have to do this."

Gerald gets to the church early and sits on the front pew alone, with his eyes fixed on the casket. "Sweet pea, I requested a closed-casket funeral so it wouldn't be so hard on the family, especially your brothers. No, that's not true—especially me. Lia is too young to fully understand what happened so we decided she shouldn't be here today." Guilt eats him up when he thinks of how he simply explained to Lia that her mommy is 'in heaven with God now, watching over you.'

He bounces his knee up and down in a failed attempt to steady his nerves. "Why didn't I pay better attention to you? You looked like you were getting better, baby. Why didn't you come to me and tell me what was going on?" Gerald gets up, leans down and hugs her coffin, then wails, "Oh, God, I don't understand. Help me understand this, please?"

Benjamin goes from kneeling to sitting with his legs crossed in front of Celeste's grave. "I thought coming home was the right thing to do, now you'll never get to see Lia grow up. He looks up to the sky. "Watching Gerald look so defeated today at your funeral . . . I had to get out of there. It was too much knowing all of this is my fault. Once again I'm fucking up his life and causing everyone pain."

He wipes his eyes with his handkerchief. "I should have never come back here, should have never put those pictures of Landis in your mailbox. All the suffering you went through . . . I did this." He places a single red rose on her grave, then stands back up, and stuffs the handkerchief back in the pocket of his trench coat. After folding his hands in front of him and peering down at her freshly covered grave one last time, he resolves, "There's only one way to make things   better.   It's   time   .   .   .   it's   time."

PART THREE

GIVING UP THE

GHOST

Chapter Nineteen

Bridget lays one of Gerald's suits on the bed. When he comes back from the shower, he kisses her. "Thank you, baby, not just for today but for all these years. I wouldn't have made it through any of this if you weren't beside me."

"How are you for real? One thing you've mastered is putting up a good face for the outside world, but when you suffer, so do I. Tell me the truth."

Gerald sits on the bed beside her and doesn't speak for a little while. Bridget climbs behind him, kneels on the bed and massages his shoulders and back. He closes his eyes. "Sweetheart, if only you could soothe my inside as well as you do my outside. Come here." He pats his lap, Bridget acquiesces then lays her head on his chest.

"Sometimes," Gerald states, "I hear her voice and see the pain in her eyes that was there during Thanksgiving dinner. Instead of going off on her I should've just . . ."

"Stop." Bridget looks him directly in the eyes. "You are not the reason Celeste . . . did that. Please, I pray day and night that you'll stop blaming yourself, Gerald." She stands up and places her hands on his shoulders. "Are you ready for this first trial? We'd all understand if you didn't go since we buried her only a week ago."

"Jet, there's no way in hell I'm letting Landis get the pleasure of not seeing me every damn time his ass is wheeled into the courtroom."

"Okay, the limo will be here in about half an hour so we'd better get dressed."

Gerald pulls her closer into a tight embrace. "No weapon formed against us . . ."

"Shall prosper," Bridget replies.

"**All rise**," The bailiff commands, as the judge enters and he announces her name. Landis still hasn't looked in the direction of the

116

prosecutor's desk where Trey and Gerald sit. Once everyone is seated and the judge states why they're there, Landis' lawyer says, "If it would please the court." The judge grants her privilege to speak.

"Thank you, Your Honor. My client, Landis Omari Faber, wishes to change his plea at this time."

The courtroom rings out with sighs, mumbles and gasps. The judge bangs her gavel. "Counselor?"

"Yes, Your Honor. The defendant would like to change his plea from not guilty, by reason of temporary insanity to guilty, and will not contest your ruling on the matter." The courtroom erupts with chatter, and news reporters can be heard in the hallway making their usual ranting.

Gerald and Trey look at one another, then over at Landis. He never raises his head.

"Order, I will have order in this court!" The judge bangs the gavel once more. When the room and hallway settle down she addresses the defending attorney. "State your reasoning, counselor."

"Your Honor, we had no indication from my client of the urgency to change his plea until right before we entered the courtroom. I never had a chance to discuss it with the prosecutor. Mr. Faber would like to make a statement, if you'll allow."

"We have no objections to that, Your Honor," The prosecutor states.

"So granted, but don't turn this into an even bigger circus, young man," The judge demands.

Landis heaves a sigh. "Your Honor, I am guilty. The plea for insanity was me being a coward as usual, and not wanting to face the consequences of my actions. A little over a week ago I received message that . . . my wife committed suicide." His eyes get glazy and his lawyer wipes them with a tissue. "A day later I received this letter in the mail and would like to read it at this time."

The judge nods yes. The people in the courtroom and reporters outside fall into silence. Trey glares at Landis like he wants to kill him. Gerald puts his arm around his son's shoulders and whispers, "Let's listen, okay?"

The defending attorney sits, holds the letter up in front of Landis and he begins:

"Landis, all I wanted was to love and be loved in return by a man as honorable as my father. You presented yourself as such, and that's why I married you. I gave you everything you said you needed, especially our beautiful baby girl. Lia gives me so much joy, but lately this monster you have become has stolen so much from me, she is not even capable of bringing it back." Landis chokes up and his lawyer puts a straw in his mouth for a sip of water before he continues.

"I'm not doing this because of embarrassment or what people will or are thinking or saying because I don't give a damn about that. But this bleeding so much inside, babe; the only way I see to stop the hemorrhage is this. Why couldn't you love me right? All I wanted was to get away from the kind of marriage my parents had, but here I am in the same shit! Living a lie, and not even aware of it until now, after someone gets killed. I'm going to end this today. I need rest. I'm going to lie down now and finally get some. Goodbye. Celeste"

119

His attorney folds the letter up and Landis looks at the judge.

His face is flushed. "My actions"—he clears his throat—"caused me to lose the movement of my body from the neck down, and the death of two women I admired and loved. Now it's time for me to man up and take responsibility for them. Please, send me to prison."

"You son-of-a-bitch, whoever shot you should have done it right!" Gerald leaps up. Walter grabs him and tries to calm him down, as the judge hammers her gavel. No one is paying attention to Trey who runs over, tackles and knocks Landis out of the wheelchair, then starts pummeling him.

"Trey, stop, please," Bridget screams, "You're going to kill him."

Complete chaos erupts in the courtroom. Benjamin watches it all from the bench furthest back. After the police grab Trey and handcuff him, Benjamin leaves.

Chapter Twenty

"Celeste killed . . . I can't even say it out loud." Tears hug Benjamin's rheumy eyes as he continues to stare at the infamous portrait that once greeted every guest who walked into what they called the 'great room'. Gerald has had the portrait removed and replaced with his office furniture. Now it's leaning up against the mansion's basement wall. Benjamin speaks to it as if his parents are there in the flesh. "I know you cussing me out right now." He looks up into his mother's eyes. "You never liked the woman, mama, but she's where I start because I'm banking on her having some love left in her heart for me . . . just pray it's enough with all I put her through."

He moves his gaze over to his father's eyes. "Pops, you know how I got in here, right, ha, ha. Me and Gerald snuck in and out, and snuck girls in and out of this basement so many times. Glad you never told mama." He lets his mind wander back to a better time in the Lamar Family's life.

"He didn't even change the alarm code, but that's your boy, always practical. I thought I'd have to search and find this big ass picture of y'all since Gerald and Bridget live here now, but as soon as I step through the basement door, here you are staring at me, old man. Felt like old times again. Let me stop revealing secrets before mama gives you that look; you remember that look. Hell, we all do. If this ole, huge, beautiful mansion could talk, she'd have put us all out before me and Gerald graduated high school." He lets out a hearty laugh, then his face gets an abstemious look.

"I'm struggling, ya'll." Benjamin puts his hands in his pockets and bows his head. "Seems like my trying to make things right turned G's world into a nightmare we all have to suffer, again.

"Listen, I'd better get going before I miss my flight. Same as always though, I got my hand out for money. Damn shame everyone is wealthy now but me. Anyway that doesn't matter; money don't mean a thing to me anymore." He stares at his father's face again. "I don't know how to pull this off, Pops, but can hear you telling me to do whatever needs to be done to fix what I fucked up." He smiles up at his mother's picture. "You didn't know about what I'm getting ready to do right now but take that up with Pops."

Benjamin reaches up, grabs the top of the portrait's frame and guides it slowly until it is face-down on the basement floor. He pulls a flathead screwdriver out of his backpack and begins removing the large staples from the back of the frame. Once they're all off he pulls the back covering off and reveals a rather large, rectangular package taped securely against the frame's midsection. "Whew, I'm glad it's still here." He cuts the tape then picks up the weighty package. "This is the last loan I take from you, old man."

"May I help you?" the receptionist asks Benjamin, without looking up from her computer.

"Yes, ma'am. I have a 4 o'clock appointment with Dr. Lamar, and you have the prettiest big, brown eyes I've ever seen." Benjamin knows that will get her to raise her gaze.

The slender brunette's mouth forms an 'o' once she does look at him. She pushes her chair back and crosses her bow-shaped legs.

"May I have your name please?" Now other ladies behind the desk stop to stare. "My, my, my," one nurse, who wears blonde dreads and a blue smock says, with no shame whatsoever.

Benjamin pulls up his sexiest baritone voice. "Good evening, lovely ladies."

"Hi," the whole crew answers almost in unison.

"Benjamin Mackey, ma'am." He says to the brunette, who begins typing into the PC again, not taking her eyes off of him. She finally glances down at the monitor. "Yes, please take a seat and someone will be right with you."

"Can I be right with you?" the other receptionist says loud enough for the whole waiting area to hear, as Benjamin goes to sit. All the ladies laugh and high-five one another.

A few minutes later the same nurse with the dreads calls his name and he follows her back to an examining room. She takes her sweet time with the preliminary questions and protocol, grinning the whole time. "Okay, Dr. Lamar will be in to see you in a minute. You take care." She winks at Benjamin and giggles then leaves.

Benjamin stands and turns his back when he hears the doctor remove the chart from the door. She enters reading the information. "Mr. Mackey, I'm Dr. Lamar. It says here you're having problems with anxiety and insomnia. When did this start?" She closes the door and sits on the stool. Benjamin doesn't turn to face her nor answer her question.

"Mr. Mackey, are you all right?"

He shakes his head no, and turns around at a snail's pace. When the doctor looks up at him, she freezes, and drops the chart and pen. Benjamin takes one step and gets so close she can smell his cologne.

"Baby girl, it's really me. You're not seeing a ghost. I'm alive, for real, see?" He has a pained expression as he takes hold of her stethoscope, gently plugs it in her ears, and places the other end to his chest. "You hear that? I'm here, in the flesh."

Camilla blacks out. Benjamin catches her before she hits the floor. He picks her up, and lays her down on the examining table, as careful as he would a feather. He kisses her lips.

Camilla opens her eyes and moves so fast to get off the table she almost bumps into the wall. "Who are you? Why would you come here and make this up? I can't have this foolishness today, or any other day!"

"Camilla, it is not make believe. I am alive. It hurts me to come to you this way after so long but it can't be helped. I can't hide from those I love anymore; it's torture." He reaches down and takes her hand, then kisses the back of it like he did the first day they met. "It's me, baby. It's Ramon."

Camilla jerks her hand away, hauls off and punches him in the mouth so hard a trickle of blood decorates his lower lip. "Get the hell away from me! Now, get out now. How dare you? How dare you come in here like this? Get out!"

Ramon pulls a handkerchief from his coat pocket and presses it against his lip. "Baby girl."

"Stop calling me that!" The door opens and several nurses as well as a security guard stands there.

"Dr. Lamar, are you okay? What's going on; your staff is concerned and called me saying it was an emergency." The guard rests his hand on his gun and glares at Ramon.

Ramon stares down at Camilla and whispers, "I'm going to be at the Ritz downtown." He shoves the guard out of his way and heads for the front door. When he gets in his car he bangs his fists on the steering wheel. "Shit, shit, shit!"

Chapter Twenty-One

Ramon takes a long bath, dries off a little then oils his body. He throws a blanket on the hotel floor, lies down and stretches out, naked. "I touched you, kissed you. You looked straight into my eyes and I saw the remnant of love. You've gotta give me a chance to explain. What we shared was more than physical, it was true." He picks up the remote, turns the channel to slow, old school R & B and closes his eyes. As The Dells' smooth, pretty harmony of *Stay In My Corner* floats into the room, the hotel phone rings.

"Hello."

No one answers.

"Camilla, I know this is you. Please say something."

"Why did you do it . . . to me, to Gerald, Bridget. Do you know the heartache you put Trey and Celeste through? Your mother died from heartbreak. Why, Rah?"

"Come to me; let me try to make you understand. All I'm asking for is a little grace, please."

"It took me a couple of years to get my mind, hell my life back in order, and the whole time you were where? This is so . . . sick." Her voice cracks. "Celeste is de—"

"I know and haven't eaten or slept much since visiting her grave. Give me a chance to make it better, please."

After a few minutes of silence Camilla says, "Open the door."

Ramon takes a deep, long breath, pulls an oversized towel from the bathroom and drapes it around his waist. He lowers the TV volume before pulling the doorknob.

Camilla steps back, takes a slow perusal of his body from head to toe, puts her hands on her head and shakes it back and forth. "It can't be you. It just can't . . ."

Ramon stretches his shivering hands out to her, as they stare into one another's eyes. "Touch me. You heard my heartbeat and saw blood on my face. I'm not a figment of your imagination. It's me, precious."

Camilla moves closer to him and places her hands on top of his. He puts them on the sides of his face. Her breathing gets arduous. Ramon steps back and holds the door open. Camilla's eyes stay glued to his as she enters. "There's only one way I'll believe this is real." She reaches up and wraps her arms around his neck.

Ramon's world stands still as he hoists her up so her legs straddle his waist. His lips tremble as they kiss and a thirst he's suffered for almost a decade is quenched.

He lays her down on the bed and Camilla begins tearing her clothes off like a mad woman, until he grabs her. "No, no. There's no need to rush this. I have to savor every sweet minute because this will be the last time, baby girl. We've gotta get this out of our system, then let it go, for the sake of everyone's sanity, including ours."

Camilla nods her head affirming, then stands on the side of the bed, as Ramon sits and gingerly undresses her. His hands are still trembling. "You have no idea how agonizing it was dreaming of holding you again, never knowing if I would," he whispers.

He moves his back up against the headboard, puts his hands on her buttocks and lifts her. Touching her reignites yearnings he thought had long passed. As she eases her body down onto his rock hard manhood and begins slow gyrations, Camilla's tears multiply. "Oh, oh! Rahhh. . . baby! Mm . . . Mm . . . Ramon!" She rocks her pelvis faster as he matches her movements with his. They go from one position to another for what seems like forever, yet not long enough.

"Camilla!" He flips her onto her back and their gyrations get harder and more rapid. "Baby girl, ohhhh shit, shit!"

She screams when he sucks her nipple as they orgasm together. Ramon slams his fist up against the headboard; his body convulses and with jagged breathing he whispers in her ear, "I'm . . . alive!"

A few hours later, Camilla awakens and quickly sits straight up in the bed.

Ramon is sitting in the chair across the room, staring at her. *Please, God, don't let her be an illusion.*

"How long did I sleep?"

"Awhile. I figured you needed that rest, so didn't wake you." He goes over and sits facing her on the bed. "Your love is what's kept me going."

She takes her index finger and traces the scars on his upper chest. "Tell me."

"It's so difficult to talk about," Ramon bites her earlobe.

"Rah, tell me." She kisses his scars and lies back down.

Ramon climbs between her legs and lays his head on her belly. "Okay."

Chapter Twenty-Two

December 2003

"I'm no fool so don't talk to me like one," Shelia Lamar shouts at FBI detective, Calvin Gold. She'd flown into Atlanta to meet with Gold and Ramon. They're in her hotel room.

"Mama, calm down, please. The man is just trying to explain," Ramon tells her.

Shelia fixes her eyes on Ramon. "I'm not stupid, son and you know it. Blank ammunition wounds can hurt like fire to your chest. This can be fatal, especially at the range you're speaking of. I just don't like it and insist you formulate a better plan."

"I'm sorry, Mrs. Lamar, but there is no better plan," Gold replies. "Ramon has committed crimes that should put him away for life, but he's chosen to witness against several other major perpetrators, including Police Chief Sinclair, in exchange for his freedom. His only choices are prison or this."

"Mama." Ramon pulls his mother's wheelchair closer to his seat, and strokes her face. "I'm not going to die or go to prison. This is my time to get out of the game, and live a halfway decent, normal life. Isn't that what you wanted?" He plants a kiss on both of Shelia's cheeks.

She stares at him shaking her head for a couple of minutes. "I'm . . . you just keep disappointing me. I come here to meet with you, not knowing why, and get a ton of bricks landed on me. It's too overwhelming." She blots her eyes with a lacy handkerchief. "Between those despicable pictures of you and Camilla, and this, I don't understand why you . . . are like this. What did we do to make you like this?"

Ramon's fair-skinned face reddens. "Nothing, mama, you and dad were fantastic parents. I don't know. It was too enticing for awhile—the money, power, it was easy for me to get and I craved it. Lately I've been exhausted and the thrill is gone. I'm telling you this, dear, because you're the one person I couldn't stand not talking to ever again. You have to keep this on the low, though. Everyone else has to believe I'm gone. Please forgive me and let me do this so I can know how it feels to sleep again."

"When?" Shelia asks.

Gold responds, "Tonight. It's all set up. Carlton Kendall is working undercover in Chief Sinclair's precinct and switched all of her service weapon's ammo to blanks. Let's pray she doesn't check the magazine closely before going to Ramon's shop. Carl let it slip out of his mouth to Shirley that Ramon and Camilla hook up every Friday night at his main business location. Our informant, Lonny Harry, told us Sinclair plans to get there a couple hours before them and hide out. Well that's what she told him; hope it's good info."

Ramon shakes his head. "That fucker Lonny. I still can't believe he's been snitching all this time."

"Well, I'm going back to Dallas," Shelia announces. "The thought of being in this city when all of that occurs is already making me crazy. Please let me know when you need me to make these fake funeral arrangements. I don't want this, Ramon. You think this will be better but the only person who gains from this is you." She weeps in her hands.

Ramon picks Shelia up out of her wheelchair, carries her to the bed and sits her there. He sits beside her and lays his head on her shoulder. "Gold, this is when you leave. Don't let the doorknob hit you. I need these final moments with my best friend," Ramon says.

"All this lying," Shelia tells Ramon once Gold leaves. "You have me doing all this lying. Your father would be livid! This isn't how we envisioned life for you, nowhere near it."

"I know, dear; you've always loved me too much. More than I've ever deserved."

Camilla gasps. "Oh my goodness. She knew, you all's mother knew about everything?"

Ramon repositions himself in the bed so they're looking straight into one another's eyes and pulls Camilla's legs around his waist. "She didn't know Shirley was her daughter. Shit, none of us saw that coming. Mama was giving me what I wanted. She always put me before her own well-being, and I was the selfish fuck-up who acted like that was what she was *supposed* to do."

After he and Camilla shower together, Ramon orders room service and they sit in silence, fully clothed, as they eat. Once the meal is finished and they're sipping red wine Ramon continues with details.

"The FBI crew were in a van down the street listening to everything."

"Rah!"

"I'm sorry, baby girl. That was the only way we saw it happening. Shirley was so jealous of you she threatened to drop a dime on me and I couldn't have that. Nobody outsmarted Rah-Money, right?"

"Why were you screwing her too?" Once the question was in the air Camilla wishes she hadn't ask. "Wait, don't answer. That's not important now."

"I used people. Back then all I wanted to do was succeed at being omnipotent. My head was so screwed up." He massages his temples. "It was all a set up, baby. I knew Shirley was in the closet and made sure she saw me put my vest in the gym bag. What I didn't know was if she'd checked her clip. None of us knew. It felt like a game of Russian fucking roulette for me. Mama was right though. All I had on was that thin undershirt. When Shirley shot got-damn blanks into my chest that close up, my ass hit the floor hard and blood started oozing.

"As soon as Gold got wind of the call Shirley made by payphone reporting shots coming from my shop, they went to work. He set up that crime scene in about 15 minutes, and then hit me with a needle that knocked my ass out. I was glad because that shit felt like hot coal to my chest."

"So it was all contrived?"

"Every bit of it, except you, Shirley, Gerald and most of Sinclair's officers. Carl was a main player in the whole scheme. That motha was good at it; I gotta give it to him."

Camilla stands and walks over to look out of the window. Ramon comes up from behind and slips his arms around her waist. "It's a lot to digest. I'm sorry. You have to know, it was the hardest thing I'd ever done in my life—leaving you." He kisses her neck. "My love was never contrived." They sway back and forth and take in the view of the Atlanta skyline.

Camilla's cell phone rings. "I gotta take this," she tells him, after looking at the number. "It's Trey."

She sits back down at the table and answers, "Hello, honey."

"Ma, somebody kidnapped Little Tip, snatched him from daycare today!"

"What?"

Chapter Twenty-Three

"How does this happen at a private daycare? All that money Uncle Tip is paying and there wasn't one worker watching him closely? What the hell?" Trey stands in Tip's humungous living room surrounded by police officers.

"They were watching, according to the workers and other children's statements," Chief Shaw answers. "Apparently Little Tip knew who got him because they said when he saw the person he just ran up to the van before anybody could stop him. By the time they got to him, whoever it was had grabbed, put him in and sped off."

The police have set up a station in Tip's living room for tracking all calls to and from his residence and cell phone. Gerald comes stomping into the room, with Bridget following him. "Where's my brother!"

"Dad," Trey says and hugs Gerald, then points out to the closed in side porch where Tip sits on a swing, swaying back and forth and puffing on a cigar. "He hasn't said a word to anyone since finding out. We all know that ain't good. When Uncle Tip gets quiet . . ."

"The calm before the storm," replies Gerald.

"More like before the Tsunami," Chief Shaw interjects. "Me and Tip don't have two good words for one another, but I want to find the youngster because this is f'd up and Collier's going to end up killing someone if we don't."

"And Mama Claudette?" Bridget enquires.

Trey answers, "Ma C's upstairs, trying to rest; the doctors gave her something for her nerves. She was going ballistic, blaming herself for not keeping Little Tip home today."

Bridget takes Gerald's coat and hat. "I'll go check on her. We left Lia with the nanny," she sighs. "This is way too much . . . Lord help our family. What a Christmas season we're having."

When Gerald walks out to the porch, Tip glances in his direction, then keeps swinging. Gerald stands in front of him so the swing halts. Tip peers up at him. "You know I'm ready."

"Tip."

"Don't go there, man, we're talking about my child. I'm gone fuck up somebody real good. All I need is a name and I'll find their ass." He hands Gerald a folded piece of copy paper. "You see this shit?"

Gerald opens the typed note and reads: *"Your son for 10, and don't play with me, bitch. No cops involved. I'm calling you at 7:00. Pick up the phone after one ring or he's dead."*

Tip stares out into his yard. "The only reason I called Shaw was 'cause mama was losing her mind. Hell, you know I don't need no help from damn law enforcement, never have."

Gerald sits beside him on the swing. "Ten million, what the fuck?"

"I already made arrangements."

Gerald shakes his head. "Big brother, come on now. You're not giving them that money."

"Yeah, but they won't live long enough to spend it. All I need is a name." He looks over at Gerald. "This is all me, okay? I need you to stay here, and stay alive."

Gerald stretches his arms out over the back of the swing. "You're talking crazy. Everybody knows Tip gets, he don't get got."

Tip purses his lips, looks up at the darkening sky and exhales smoke. "My son . . . my only child, G. If I have to give my life to keep him from being hurt, not even a second thought. Every damn dime I got is for my boy. He's the reason I get out of bed every morning." He focuses his eyes on one of Little Tip's bikes that leans on the side of the porch, draws in and blows out another cigar drag. "Not even a second thought."

Gerald pats his brother's shoulder. "I know, man."

Bridget goes into one of Tip's guest bedrooms and shuts the door. She sits on the bed, closes her eyes and lets her tears flow. "Dear God, please don't let this happen. We've lost so much already this year, too much. Little Tip has to be so scared right now. He's lost his mother, then Celeste, finally met and lost his grandfather all in the past few months. That poor baby! Please, no more, Lord. Amen."

Chapter Twenty-Four

At 7 PM everyone is sitting in the living room, including several police officers with recording devices and laptops in front of them. Tip's cell phone rings once. He picks it up and puts on speakerphone

"Where the fuck is my son?"

"Daddy!"

Tip's shoulders drop. "Little man, where are you?"

"I don't know," Little Tip cries. "He won't tell me."

"You all right? Are you hurt? Who is he, son?"

"No, stop it. Let me talk to my daddy!"

The phone goes silent for a moment and Tip begins a frantic pace from one side of the room to the other. He stops abruptly when he hears a voice he knows all too well.

"Who's the motherfucker now?"

Tip and everyone else in the room gets totally still.

"Amos, you raggedy ass, freeloading, bitch ho! I'm going to put you in the grave right beside your benefactor!"

"That's all fine and good, but try that 'Shaft' shit with me, and you'll be burying this little monster of yours the same day. Now calm your old gangster ass down, before I change my mind."

"I'm coming to get my son," Tip says, "then I'm gone send your ass to hell."

"Well, I'll wait on you to meet me there," Amos retorts. "But until then you need to put 10 million in a safety deposit box at the bank tomorrow before noon. The information will be sent to you in a text message in about a minute or so. I'll give you further instructions on where to pick up this little brat after I collect my money."

"You don't know me, boy, you just think you do. I'm surprised Shirley didn't get you up on the game, but you will be dead sooner than you think or imagine. Everyone who knows me knows I ain't one to be played with."

"Bitch, fuck you and Shirley! It's because of her that this is even necessary. I had Josiah all to myself, and was working my hustle to be set up good for the rest of my life. When he found that loony heifer, I became an afterthought. Shit, I'm not even gay, love me some pussy, the more the better; but whatever Daddy Warbucks needed to get his limp dick up, I provided. Thinking the whole time he'd leave me right. That was my grind, and you know what that old bastard left me—not. a. damn. thang. Every freaking dollar and piece of property was willed to this little son-of-a-bitch! So as far as I'm concerned, y'all owe me for my services and I aims to get paid."

Click

Before anyone could get to him Tip throws the phone down, stomps and grinds it with his foot. "I hope the phone call didn't get traced because I want all of you out of my house!" Gerald rushes to stand beside him.

"We didn't get it, Collier," Chief Shaw confirms.

"Good, now leave, Jack."

"You sure about this, come on," Shaw pleads. "There's no need for you to put your life on the line if we can prevent it. Think about what you're doing?" He looks at Tip with sincerity in his eyes. "I have three sons, and if this was me, I'd feel the same way, but let me help you. We can do this together."

Claudette comes over to where they're standing and slips her hand into Tip's. "Patrick?"

"Mama, don't ask me, please."

"Boy, you always so stubborn, you and that child are all I got left of blood kin. You think about who is going to take care of me and him when you go out there and get yourself killed?"

"Mama . . . you know I can't let Amos get aw—"

Claudette slaps his face hard. "Look at me!" He looks at her like she lost her mind. "You don't want to lose your son," she tells him, "well, I don't want to lose mine. Now you let the law help you, hear me? I want both my son and grandson to come back to this house living and whole."

Tip kisses the back of his mother's hands. "How you wait until I'm 52 to finally hit me?" He smiles down at her.

Claudette doesn't return the smile. "It wouldn't have worked then, looks like not now either. You just gone do what your mind is set on."

"I have to, sweetie. But one thing I can promise is to grant your request. Everything I have in my power will be utilized to bring me and Little Tip home safely."

Claudette points in Bridget's direction. "Child, come help me back upstairs," she tells her. "I just want my sweet baby home, that's all. He sounded so fragile on the phone."

Her tears swell the tightness that's been gripping Tip's chest since Little Tip was abducted. "Mama," he whispers, before collapsing to the floor.

Chapter Twenty-Five

The veins in Gerald's neck look like they're about to explode as he watches Tip lie in an ICU hospital bed with tubes flowing from his body. Bridget and Trey sit in the waiting area trying to eat a little of the breakfast Marcus has brought them.

"Ma, what happens now with lil cousin? Uncle Tip was the one supposed to drop that money. What we gonna do?" Marcus asks.

Bridget rubs up and down her arms. "I don't know, baby. This is all just too much . . . so much."

"I'm going to take care of it." They all look up and Gerald is standing there. Bridget opens her mouth to protest and he looks at her with his face contorted in anger. "Nobody will die, not Tip, me, nor Little Tip." He hovers over them and takes turns staring each one in the eye. "The fortunate thing is Tip's phone took a beating, but still works so I retrieved the text message last night. The bank is in Atlanta and I am going alone."

This time Bridget does speak. "No you're not."

Gerald's nostrils flare. "The plane is geared up, Jet. This is one time when I'm putting my foot down. You stay here. Claudette needs you here, understand. No more discussion."

"At least let me go with you," Trey requests.

"What part of no more discussion do y'all not comprehend. My brother is lying in a damn hospital bed unconscious and his son is God knows where being traumatized. I'm going alone. Got it? Trey, you are needed here."

Trey looks up at him and nods. Marcus stands and is almost eye-to-eye with Gerald. "Dad," he says while their eyes are fixed on one another. "You coming back, right? I mean,"—he puts his hands in his pockets and shifts his feet—"you know."

Gerald grabs him and they hold on to one another for a few minutes, then he whispers in Marcus' ear, "I'm coming back, boy, don't you go doubting that for a minute, okay? You take care of your mom while I'm gone."

Bridget gets up, puts her hand on her hip and walks out into the hall. Gerald follows her to an empty lounge.

"Have you lost your mind?"

"What the hell you expect me to do, woman?"

"What Tip wouldn't, let law enforcement handle this. You don't even know if Tip is going to recover. He had a massive heart attack, massive! And you're just going to up and fly to another city, put your life in danger? I'm tired of losing people . . . I'm tired."

Gerald pulls her close to his chest. "Listen, when this was reversed and I was lying up in the hospital, Tip didn't hesitate to go looking for Shirley's crazy ass, remember? Now, I know you're afraid, baby, but you can't talk me out of this. I'm going to put that money in the safety deposit box, and wait for Amos to say where he's dropping off Little Tip, then we're coming home. That's what's getting ready to happen." He cups Bridget's face with his hands and plants a passionate, lengthy kiss on her lips. "I will be back."

Three hours later Gerald sits in a coffee shop on Ponce de Leon Avenue in Atlanta. The 10 million sits in the designated safety deposit box. Tip's cell phone dings indicating the receipt of a text message and Gerald reads:

151

"It's good doing business with ya. I'm holding on to the prize for another 5. Seeing as how easy it was for you to come up with the 10. No back talk just put that shit in the box by 2:00 tomorrow."

Gerald bites down so hard his jawbones pulsate; he texts back, **"You, piece of shit, just crossed a line that ends with your toe tagged."**

Ramon sits in a sports bar in Midtown Atlanta, wearing shades and baseball cap. His goal is to grab a bite to eat and head back to Dallas that evening. Staying on his old stomping grounds too long heightens the chance of somebody recognizing him. He is about to chomp down on a Philly cheese stake sub when he looks up and sees Gerald, the Atlanta police chief and mayor on the big screen. "Hey, excuse me, sir," he addresses the bartender. "You mind turning that up, please?"

The bartender obliges and Ramon glues his eyes on the TV. The screen goes half-in-half with the police chief live on one side and a picture of Little Tip on the other.

"Citizens of Atlanta," the chief states, "the nephew of one of our finest former police lieutenants, Gerald Lamar, who is standing here with me, was kidnapped yesterday. We are asking that anyone who knows or has seen this man,"—a picture of Amos replaces Little Tip's—"please notify authorities immediately. Do not try to apprehend him yourself as that will put the child in even more danger.

"Amos Banks has a long criminal record and is armed and extremely dangerous. Our department is using every available officer to hunt down and capture Banks. We will find him. Mr. Lamar would like to say few words at this time."

Gerald steps to the podium with a blank expression on his face and looks directly into the camera.

"Amos, I know you're looking at this. The best thing you can do for yourself right now is leave my nephew somewhere and let me know where. If one hair is harmed on his head, you'll still be tracked down like a rabid dog."

Ramon rushes out of the bar.

Chapter Twenty-Six

"So you know this man?" Camilla and Ramon are sitting on a bench in Piedmont Park.

Ramon stretches his legs out and starts picking at his fingernails.

Camilla pulls off her knitted scarf, then puts it on tighter to cover her earlobes. "Rah, the only time you used to do that was when your mind was reeling a mile a minute," she says. "Talk to me."

He looks off into the distance. "He was one of the youngest dope boys I had on the corners." He adjusts his stocking cap and rubs his gloved hands together. "When we met he was 10 years old and crying in a parking lot, all dirty and smelling because his crack-ho mama had abandoned him. By the time I got out of the business, Amos was around 19 and one of my best sergeants."

"Wow."

"Yep, another life I fucked up." Ramon puts his hands in his pockets. "So now I have to find and probably kill him."

Camilla turns her head. "You know I can't hear that." She gets up and starts to walk off but Ramon pulls her arm.

She looks at him with her eyes squinted into slants and chest rapidly rising and falling. "Kill him like you did my brother?"

Ramon pulls her down onto his lap. "That was a different me, a selfish, arrogant, narcissistic, bullshit artist, who thought everyone should bow down to him. There's nothing I can do to change my past and you have every damn right to leave here today and never have another fucking thing to do or say to me. Please don't though, please." He smoothes her hair back with his hand. "Right now you're my only family connection."

Camilla rubs his beard with the back of her hand. "I gotta go. I know you'll do what you think is right under these circumstances, but if we're to remain close, don't tell me things like that in the future. Our daughter just died." She shuts her watery eyes. "No more talk of death, okay."

Ramon kisses her cheek. "All right, but I'm going to bring Tip's son home by any means necessary and once Amos sees me . . . there's only one way for it to end. That's how I raised him to be."

Over the next 24 hours, Ramon ducks and dodges police as he slips in and out of areas where he'd established safe houses as a kingpin. Some of the places are abandoned or demolished now, but this one particular underground spot Ramon suspects is still more than likely hot. He's sure the cops have no clue about this hideaway and most of them never come into the neighborhood at all.

"Bingo," he says when around midnight Amos walks up to street level with another fellow who looks around 16 or 17 years old. Ramon shakes his head as Amos disappears, leaving the other young man on the street. "I think I'll go buy me a taste."

He pulls his knitted cap down, and wraps a black scarf around his neck and mouth. With his hands in his jeans pockets he walks across the street to the dealer, looks around acting fidgety, and slips him 2 C notes. "Eight ball?" Ramon whispers.

"Fifty mo." The dealer keeps his gaze straight forward.

"What?"

"Yeah, fool, so give it up? You taking too long, stupid ass motherf—"

Quick as a flash Ramon puts a chokehold on him and a gun to his head, the whole time looking around to make sure no more hoods are lurking. "What do they call you?"

"Monster."

"Monster, I want you to listen carefully to everything I say and do as you're told."

Monster raises his hands and shakes his head up and down.

"Good boy, now, ease that 9 out of your coat pocket, and don't act like this is *The Wire* 'cause that was television. You're fucking with the real life original gangster right now. Try and pull up on me if you want to die tonight. That's left up to you." The young man hands Ramon the gun.

"All right," Ramon says, "Nice and slow like, walk back down these steps and use that coded knock."

"Man, fuck you. If you gonna kill me do it. I ain't goin' out like no biotch."

Ramon turns the chokehold into a sleeper and Monster goes down, out for the count. He puts the 9 in his waistband, then pulls a sawed off shotgun from beneath his trench coat and blasts the lock off basement door. People in the neighborhood start running for cover and locking their doors like it's normal everyday activity.

When he walks in he's greeted by darkness, as he knows he would be. "A-Moe, come out, come out, wherever you are."

Ramon squats, reaches under the carpet, flips the hidden light switch. Blue light envelops the room and Amos stands in the middle of the floor pointing a Glock at him. His face almost turns as white as bleached-flour.

"Ain't but one man who would know about that switch besides me. Rah, is that you? What the fuck!" Amos cocks his gun, and Ramon quickly jumps behind a corner, while firing one shot to Amos's kneecap. Amos tumbles to the floor, screaming obscenities.

"You can't win against ya master, A-Moe, stop trying," Rah says. "I'm disappointed in you for being here alone, thought I was gonna blow about seven or eight motherfuckers away. You ruined my high, boy. Didn't I teach you better?"

While Ramon is talking Amos pulls himself up and hops on one leg to a barstool, hollering like a baby from the pain. "I knew you wasn't dead! Back then I kept telling all them mofos that, but no, they wouldn't believe me. You wouldn't have gone out like that. I knew it!"

Ramon takes a deep breath."Put the gun down. Come on, I don't want to kill you or anybody else. Just here for the boy."

"Ohhh, shit, shit," Amos screams as blood oozes out of where his kneecap once was. He coughs and wipes his nose with the back of his hand. "You'll be proud of me, Rah. This is the first time I've ever been shot. You taught me right."

Ramon puts is back straight up against the wall and closes his eyes. "I know, but you gotta give me that child so I won't kill you. You're like my son and it shouldn't end like this."

"Just do it!"

"Cops will be here in a minute, just give me Tip's son and you live."

"Live for what, huh?"

"Amos . . ."

"Got-damn!" Amos yells. The pain is so excruciating he starts heaving. "You left me, man. The crew fell apart without you. I thought I was ready but . . . wasn't and ended up having to get

159

money in a desperate way to keep up my lifestyle. B-But now, I got some high quality product coming, okay." He coughs. "We can build your kingdom again, like old times."

Ramon comes from out of the shadows with his gun trained on Amos. "I'm not that person anymore. Don't make me do this, A-Moe," Ramon pleads. "You're losing so much blood now; in a few minutes you'll be unconscious."

Sweat drips like rain down Amos's face and his teeth chatter. "Y-you look good. Older, b-but still good." Amos winces. "One of us is going to die in a minute so I want to say thanks, Rah, for rescuing me from rock bottom a-and for a little while allowing me to see what it's like to live large. We were ballin', man. I . . . really been missing you. Aw, fuck!"

"Amos, put down your gun, son. I'm begging you."

Amos's eyes get as wide as saucers. "No!" He pulls the trigger and the bullet misses Ramon's face within an inch.

Ramon blasts a whole in Amos's chest with the shotgun. Amos slumps over and falls out of the chair. When Ramon turns around he bows to his knees. Amos has saved his life. Monster is lying in the doorway with a gun in his hand, and a gaping hole in his head. "No time for regrets, finish the job," he tells himself, then drags Monster's body away from the exit.

Ramon rushes to the back room where he finds Little Tip crying uncontrollably, with his hands and feet bound and mouth taped. He grabs the boy, throws him over his shoulder and sprints for the door. Ramon runs down a dark alleyway to his pickup. He opens the door and pushes Little Tip into the cab, then gets in, backs out and speeds off.

Chapter Twenty-Seven

Gerald, Camilla and Little Tip walk into Tip's hospital room where he's sitting up, with his mother holding one hand and Bridget the other. When Little Tip climbs in bed with him, there's not a dry eye in the room. Tip raises his bed up a little more, bear-hugs his son and holds on tight.

"Let's give them a moment," Claudette says after kissing both Tip and Little Tip on the cheek. She lifts her hands up toward the ceiling. "Father, God, I thank you. Amen."

"Amen," responds the others in the room.

When they're alone, Little Tip rubs his nose against Tip's. "Dad, you can stop crying now." He smirks.

"Boy, hush." Tip tickles him. "When I get out of here, me and you have to talk all about what happened to you, okay? We'll talk as long or short as you want."

Little Tip's eyes droop. "Didn't mean to make you sick." He rubs his eyes. "I wasn't scared, honest. One time Amos came in that room and I kicked him in the nuts really hard, just like you taught me. That's why he tied me up."

Tip tries to keep a straight face. "No, little man, you didn't make me sick. That's all on me." He lifts his son's chin with his finger. "Your dad needs to stop smoking, and put down the liquor bottles. You should've been rescued by me, not some stranger."

"Yeah, but I know him."

"What?"

"I mean when Granny Shelia was living and I was little and would go stay with her, she had this picture at the top of the stairs. It was fun for me to climb all the way to the top so I could see it. It was Uncle Gerald and he had hair." Little Tip chuckles. "And that man. I know it was him because he has the same eyes. I used to look at that picture all the time."

Curiosity etches Tip's face. "Did Uncle Gerald and Aunty Camilla meet this man?"

"No, because what he did was drive all the way to Aunty Camilla's house—I fell asleep on the way—and told me to walk up and ring the doorbell. Then she came out and got me and then he was gone."

"All right, good buddy." Tip decides to not press the issue. He lets the head of the bed down, and Little Tip wraps himself around his father.

"I sure do love you, daddy."

Tip feels his body relax. "I love you to infinity, son."

After a couple of minutes both Tips are snoring.

A few days later Ramon's doorbell rings and when he answers Camilla is standing there wearing a beautiful African print coat and makeup to perfection, looking like a younger version of Phylicia Rashad. He invites her in. "To what do I owe the pleasure?" Ramon fails miserably at hiding his excitement.

The townhouse is only sprinkled with furniture so he pulls out a chair from a little table in his nook and offers her a seat. He sits across from her.

"You may kick me out after what I propose."

Ramon gives her a quizzical look. "Kicking you out of any space I occupy is never an option." He takes her hands in his and starts rubbing them. "You need some gloves on, lady."

Camilla gets a wistful look in her eyes. "You told me you're leaving soon. Have you decided when?"

He kisses her hands. "Are you trying to get rid of me?"

"No, nothing like that," she answers. "We agreed to always be friends, right; no more lovemaking but still love nonetheless?" Ramon leans back in his seat and folds his arms.

"Baby girl, now, as long as I've known you, you've never been one to beat around the bush with me."

"I've been agonizing over something since we lost Celeste." She pauses. "You know you can't hide forever."

"I don't plan on it. Tell me straight up what's on your mind."

"Well, there's a Christmas dinner today. We're also celebrating Tip and Little Tip both being home and . . ."

"You're inviting me to come and ruin the celebration?"

Camilla looks at him sullenly. "If not now when? Rah, no matter how, when, or where, sooner or later you're going to have to let the rest of the family know you're alive. It's never going to be pretty."

She and Ramon gaze into one another's eyes. Camilla stands and straps her purse over her shoulder. "Let's go."

"Are you crazy?" Ramon asks with a slack jawed-expression. "Look, Gerald and Bridget have buried the hatchet with you, but you're talking about springing my resurrection on them right now, after all this family has been through the past few months?"

Camilla walks to the door, stops and turns around and stares at him with a crestfallen look. "Shelia, then Celeste: how many more people have to die for you to realize you're still selfish. Tip went into cardiac arrest two weeks ago and almost died too. You're stuck on trying to fix what you fucked up, as you keep saying, without doing the one thing that could put closure to all of Gerald's suffering."

"Baby girl."

"No, it's been too many years, Rah! What we did was dead wrong, but I stayed here and took my punishment, allowed years to pass with very little contact from my children. Lost my best friend, and deserved to. It has taken me this long to get back in Trey's life and I never got to reconcile with our *baby girl*." Camilla breaks down, Ramon moves closer to comfort her.

She holds up one finger in his direction. "No more. You put your life on the line to save Tip's son, yet how much will you give to save your own? Do you know Trey lost a part of himself when he found out about us? He's spent the past nine years trying his best not to be you, when really all he ever wanted to be was like you. As a child he worshipped his Uncle Rah. I know you've seen he's almost your spittin' image." Camilla opens her purse, takes out a tissue and blots her eyes and cheeks.

Ramon reaches out and takes her hand. "I'm so sorry. That doesn't fix a thing, words are only words, but mama was right and so are you. What I've been through doesn't compare in the least bit to what I put on y'all." His shoulders slump. "Here are two words I've never uttered in my life: I'm scared."

Chapter Twenty-Eight

A jovial spirit permeates the atmosphere at the Lamar family mansion. A Christmas tree illuminates each bay window downstairs. Everyone's stomach is full of the smorgasbord Bridget prepared, and Lia and Little Tip, after playing with what seems like millions of toys they got for Christmas, are upstairs napping with Claudette. Michael Jackson belts *Santa Clause Is Coming To Town* through Bose speakers.

All the others sit in the den chatting and sipping champagne, except Tip, who has sworn off alcohol. He and Gerald talk noise as they whip Trey and Marcus in dominoes. Bridget notices Camilla's quiet demeanor. She goes over to the loveseat and eases down beside her.

"Camilla," she says for the fourth time.

Camilla shakes her head and looks at Bridget. "I'm sorry; did you say something?"

"Well I only called your name a few times." Bridget laughs. "Penny for your thoughts."

Camilla slides her hand into Bridget's and looks at her lovingly. "I'm so grateful to be sitting here with you like this again. There were many times over the years I wanted to call you. Sometimes I'd cry because I couldn't reach out to you."

Bridget grins and opens her arms. "Come on, sistah, give it up." The ladies hug. "I'm gonna tell you as many times as it takes; the past is in the past. Me and Gerald are ecstatically happy and after all we've overcome, I really believe this is how God wants it to be. Sometimes we gotta go through to get to the other side of through, know what I mean?"

"Girl, your faith is one thing I've always admired," Camilla replies. Her face goes blank and she stares into the distance again.

"Okay, what's going on in your head today for real?" Bridget asks. "I'm the one person who could always read your body language. Something's worrying you. Are you thinking about Celeste?"

Camilla squeezes Bridget's hand. "There's something I have to do, that must be done for all of our sakes. I just don't know what the fall out will be, but hearing you say Celeste's name gives me courage." As Bridget stares at her with a confused facial expression, Camilla excuses herself and walks into the kitchen. She presses the 'call' button on her cell phone and when someone answers says, "Okay, the time has come." She hangs up, goes back into the den and walks over to the table where the guys are playing dominoes.

Camilla puts her hand on Gerald's shoulder and he looks at her with a smile. "You okay?"

"Not really," She answers. "I want to say something important to everyone please, if you don't mind."

"Ma, what's the matter?" Trey doesn't like the agitated expression on Camilla's face.

She goes over, kisses him on the cheek and says, "I have to do this, baby. Please don't hold it against me. I just got you back and it would kill me to lose you again." She massages his shoulders.

Trey turns and looks at her with a frown. "You've been acting weird all day. What gives?"

Camilla asks Marcus to turn the stereo off. Bridget walks over to Gerald and stands behind him. Everyone stares at Camilla.

She takes a deep breath then exhales. "These last few months have changed me. Losing Celeste like that . . . it made me realize life's way too short. Gerald and Bridget, y'all are so good together and I'm happy, sincerely. You've been the glue holding us all in place, giving us strength to carry on. Your forgiveness is one thing I'll be thankful for the rest of my life."

Gerald speaks up with a hoarse voice. "We're good, you don't have to keep thanking us. My heart is still in pieces over Celeste, but we all have to find a way to move on; that's what she'd want."

Tip can tell some shit is about to hit the fan. "Camilla, whatever you have to say, please know my gratitude to you for bringing my boy home won't be shaken by it. Lift the weight off your mind, sweetheart."

Camilla nods and pushes play on the recorder of her phone, then sits it on the table. "Please, everyone listen carefully." She places her hands back on Trey's shoulders, bows her head and closes her eyes.

The grandfather clock ticking in the hallway is the only sound in the room until the voice of a ghost rises from Camilla's phone.

"Gerald,"— Ramon sighs heavily—*"This is not some trick or ruse. Please don't blame Camilla for anything that happens today. She's only guilty of wanting the truth finally out in the open."*

Gerald slowly rises to his feet. Bridget gazes at the phone, stunned, with her hand on her mouth.

Ramon's recording continues.

"I've put hurt and pain to the highest degree on everyone, especially you, Gerald, and I just want to . . . make it right."

Camilla stops the recording. Gerald is breathing so hard it looks like his heart is going to jump out of his chest. He glares at Camilla. "What the hell is this? How long have you had that and what does he mean 'make it right'? He can't make shit right from the grave!"

Trey stands and stares past Gerald and Bridget like he's in a trance. "Rah."

"I know that's Ramon on that tape, boy, I'm asking your mother why she felt this was the time to bring that into my home and play it when I'm finally getting back to a little peace of mind."

172

"No, dad, it's him . . . here." Trey whispers and steps to the side for a clearer view of the dead man walking.

Bridget turns and looks in the direction of Trey's stare. Her mouth drops open and she backs up into Gerald, which gets him to pivot. Then he sees him.

Ramon takes his hat off. The tears come slowly and steadily down his face, like drops of water from a melting ice sickle. "Gerald."

No one in the room moves. Gerald and Ramon eye one another without blinking, and Tip senses a bull versus matador scene about to unfold. He breaks the silence.

"Gerald." When Gerald keeps glaring at Ramon without answering, Tip walks in between the two and looks up at him. "I know you hear me, Negro." Gerald moves his gaze down to Tip, and Tip sees the volcano about to erupt. "Don't do it. It won't make anything better, man. You know it."

In a split second Gerald pushes Tip out of his way and barrels into Ramon. The both of them fall to the floor like huge oak trees. Gerald raises up and starts bashing Ramon in the face and head with his fists. "You motherfucker. You lying ass, sorry ass, conceited motherfucker, I'll kill you!"

Ramon holds his arms over his face as protection.

Trey and Marcus rush over, grab Gerald by the arms and pull him away from Ramon.

Ramon sits up and wheezes, with blood dripping from his nose. He looks up at Gerald. "I'm sorry; you gotta know I'm . . . so sorry, G."

Gerald breaks free of the stronghold his sons have on him, then hovers over Ramon. Ramon takes a handkerchief from his pocket and holds it to his nose.

"Sorry for what?" Gerald yells. "What the fuck are you sorry for, Rah! Stand up, look me in my eye and tell me exactly what you sorry for. Are you sorry for screwing my wife behind my back for 20 years? Are you sorry for knowing you fathered my children, but kept lying to my face for 20 years? Are you sorry for living a double life, while I bragged on you to everybody like a damn fool? Are you sorry for the state mama was in when she died? You used and abused her love so much. Between you and Shirley's loony ass, mama died wounded and depressed, but hell you weren't here to see that were you?"

Ramon stands staggering. Tip retrieves a chair from the table and sits it behind him. Ramon sits. He and Gerald still haven't taken their eyes off one another. "I have so much to tell you, G. Y-you gotta listen, please. Listen today and if you don't want me back in your life I'll leave forever."

Chapter Twenty-Nine

Bridget continues to stare at Ramon as if he's a spirit. Trey comes up to him and speaks barely above a whisper. "Is it really you, Uncle Rah? H-how the hell?"

Ramon puts his hand over Trey's heart. "I'm real, son, and if I could erase all the trash from my past and start over again I would, especially the betrayal and the pain I caused my children."

"Don't call them that!" Gerald's booming voice echoes throughout the room. "You have never been their father." His nostrils flare.

Ramon bows his head and it seems like no one breathes as he relays the facts of what happened before he went into witness protection.

"It was all about me. You're right, G. Back then I didn't give a damn about anybody but myself. Power and control over others was like a drug for me. But when I sat at mama's funeral—yes, I was there against the will of the powers that be—it hit me like a ton of bricks: I truly was dead. Mama was my one connection to my former life and she died; my superwoman died." He folds his handkerchief, wipes his bloody nose, and raises his gaze back up to Gerald.

"I came back because I saw you on television, looking beaten and worn, worrying over my children. I looked the marshals in the eye and told them I was taking my protection into my own hands and coming here to help you, to pay you back a little for all the shit I did." He gives every detail of what he's done since moving back to Dallas, including murdering Wells, and shooting Landis.

"He had his hands around my daughter's neck strangling the life out of her." He coughs. "I couldn't let that happen. Bitch better be happy I was only aiming to maim, not kill."

"Lord, have mercy." Bridget pulls a chair from under the table and sits down.

The tension in Ramon's body subsides some as he hears her voice. He glances at her. "You look real good, B. Always was so beautiful."

Gerald exhales like he's breathing fire. "Keep your eyes off my wife and I said do not call them your children," he tells Ramon through clenched teeth. "And now that you've told your tale, yeah, you can get back out of my home and my life." He gets in Ramon's face. "Go back to the got-damn grave before I put you there permanently."

"Uncle Gerald, no." Little Tip sprints up to Ramon, and jumps in between him and Gerald. "Don't make him leave."

"Son, get out of the way before you get hurt," Tip says sternly. "Come here, right now."

Little Tip shakes his head. "No, sir." He pulls on Gerald's shirt. "Please don't be mean to him, he saved my life. The way he handled up on Amos was awesome; it was straight up sick. I mean, he's da man!"

Tip can't do anything but shake his head and chuckle.

Little Tip turns to Ramon and raises both hands for a high-five, but quickly lowers them back to his side; his face reddens. "What is all that blood from? Did somebody punch you?"

The room gets completely quiet again.

Marcus pulls on Little Tip's hand. "Come on man, this is grown folks business. He lifts the boy up and puts him on his shoulders. "We'll go watch your favorite movie, okay?" He leaves the room and heads downstairs to the home-studio.

"Yay, *Transformers.*" Little Tip throws both fists into the air.

When they're out of earshot Tip walks up to Gerald and shoves him in the chest. "You need to calm the fuck down right now." He turns to the others. "I know you all want to keep staring at Ramon like he's *The Brother From Another Planet,* but won't nothing get fixed until Gerald and Ramon have a man-to-man conversation.

"I'm going to stick around to referee. No disrespect Bridget, because this is your home, but please leave me alone with these two for about an hour or so." He winks at Bridget.

Bridget gets up, goes over to Ramon. "You look good too." She smiles and stretches her hand out. Take off your coat and hand me your dress shirt. I'll wash it for you—get that blood out."

He removes both items and gives them to her and holds on to her hands. "I'm so sorry, for everything, B. From the cheating to the lying to . . . "

Bridget puts her hand over his mouth, kisses him on the cheek and whispers in his ear, "It's all in God's hands. I forgive you, now work on forgiving yourself."

Ramon shakes his head up and down.

"Trey," Camilla says as she and Bridget exit.

Trey shakes his head no. "I'm staying. For the sake of my sanity, I need to witness what's about the happen."

Nobody argues with him.

Chapter Thirty

The men of the Lamar family all sit at the kitchen table: Gerald with an icepack laying on his right hand, Ramon with one of Gerald's shirts on, holding an icepack on his right jaw, Trey still gazing at Ramon like he's not sure what's happened in the last 30 minutes, and Tip with his legs crossed, hands clasp in his lap, wearing an expression of frustration. He has placed a manila envelope on the table.

"Y'all look like two old fools who don't know they old," he tells Gerald and Ramon. "I wish I had a mirror so you could look at yourselves."

Gerald glares across the table at Ramon, who stares back with a contrite look on his face.

After about five minutes of silence, Tip says, "Let me tell you suckers something. After all these damn years somebody needs to talk, 'cause if you don't I'm gone tell you a long story. And you better listen to it too."

Ramon lays his icepack down. "Gerald, I missed you. That is what made my life even more miserable, not having you in it. I, I can't change the past, but I have changed, man. Family means life to me now because for the last nine years I didn't have mine."

"What was all that fake crime scene for, Rah?" Gerald asks, sounding exactly like their father to Tip. "I was blubbering like a little boy all over you in front of a room full of people and most of them knew it was all a façade. Then Tip tells me he was investigating your doggish activities for Bridget and found out you were a damn drug kingpin and screwing my wife ever since you moved back to the states."

Ramon hangs his head.

"How long would it take you to get over all that shit if I had done it to you, huh? And here you come on Christmas day, years later. I'm sitting up here with my family, still mourning Celeste's suicide"—his voice cracks—"and finally having a pretty great day, then low and behold, my ex-wife announces the Rahsurrection."

"I am sorry, you . . . didn't deserve none of that, not even today, but I can't take it back. What can I do to get you to forgive me?"

"Not this."

"Dad, he almost got killed finding and saving Little Tip. Doesn't that count for some mercy?" Trey asks. "Isn't that what all that preaching you do is about?"

Gerald slams his hand on the table, and tells Trey, "Don't forget who you're talking to, boy."

"You don't think I want to bust him in the mouth too? I was a college sophomore when all that went down. You're not the only one that got messed up over that shit!" The other men all turn and look at Trey.

He puts a string of pearls on the table. "I've carried these with me ever since that night Sonya died, because I bought them for her for the wrong reason—to get her so strung out on me she wouldn't screw nobody else, while I hoed like coochie was going out of style. We had a fight about my other women and she gave the necklace back, right before getting in her car to leave.

"Celeste took her own life." He chokes up. "And in her suicide note she referred to how our mother and got-damn uncle fucked our minds all up when it comes to relationships. It's like a damn family curse."

Gerald reaches over and grabs Trey's hand. "Son."

Trey jerks his hand away and his jaw muscles clench. He lays his hands flat on the table and breathes in and out deeply a couple of times. "I'm 29 years old, and sometimes feel 20 years older because of that one year in my life. Don't ya'll get that?" He brings the volume of his voice down to normal and tells Gerald, "Uncle Rah is who I see when I look in the mirror every day. Oh, yeah, I got your ways and mannerisms, but my reflection is all him."

Ramon sits, watches and listens as he's being talked about like he's not even in the room. His face gets flushed and heart rate increases. He stands. "Um, it's best if I leave. This wasn't the right way to, hell I don't know if there is a right way to return from the dead, but at least now y'all know. Time to go back to being Benjamin Mackey. This was a mistake; it's causing more confusion and pain. That's not what I wanted at all." He looks at Gerald. "I'm out, G. Like you said, Rah belongs in the grave."

Tip glowers at Ramon with piercing steel-green eyes. "Sit down."

"Tip, this was the wrong thing to do," Ramon replies.

"I said sit your ass down. It's my turn to talk. Let me give you three a *'Once Upon A Time'* tale. Only this one is true."

Chapter Thirty-One

April 1982

"You don't get to judge me, boy." Tip's father's eyes flicker like green flames. "You're my flesh and blood, my oldest son and I took damn good care of you all your life, didn't I? What gives you the right to judge me?"

Twenty-two year old Tip glares up at Gerald Lamar Sr. "Judge you? I'm not sure who the hell you are."

"I'm the man that's fed, clothed, put a roof over your head all your days on earth and paid for you to go to one of the finest historic black institutions of higher learning in this country."

"You're stalling. Just tell me the truth, dad."

"The truth is this is none of your damn business," Gerald Sr. quips.

"You gave me a fake ass name. I'd say that is my business, and what is mama to you, a side piece?"

Gerald Sr. slams his fist on the table and points in Tip's face, his hand shakes. "You say that shit to me one more time and I'll beat you within an inch of your life!"

Tip throws a folder on the table, pulls out pictures of Shelia, Gerald Jr. and Ramon. "You summoned me here like you were ready to lay it all out on the table, well look down, dad. I just did. Since you refused to tell me anything the other day I kept searching for more answers. Do you want me to tell you what I found, or are you going to tell me?"

His father takes a seat beside him and picks up the photos. He presses Shelia's picture against his lips. "You won't understand," he says. "It was love at first sight for Claudette and me. Your mother is the heartbeat of my existence, but Shelia is the reason I'm the man I am today. She's given me her lifetime commitment, forgiven every sin and looked over every fault. Her love is strong, like a tower."

Tip fumes. "How you sitting in my mama's house, drooling over another woman like that. That's some foul ass shit. No, I don't' know who you are and . . . probably never will."

"I love them both the same, son. Some people don't think that's possible, but it is. I've lived it the last 22 years, and you have no business questioning me! Coming up in here all puffed up like you're gonna whip my ass. Boy, you done lost your mind. You need to forget you ever found this out, and never bring it up again. Am I making myself clear?"

Tip's stare is so cold it looks like he's trying to bore holes through Gerald Sr. with his eyes. "Oh it's getting clearer by the minute, father dear," he says in a calm, monotone voice. "But there's another piece of information in this file. You want me to forget that too, because I'm sure it would be interesting to your *'strong tower'* of a wife down in Dallas."

Gerald Sr. rises from the table, grabs Tip by the shirt collar, pulling him out of his seat, and slams him against the wall. He speaks in a gruff, almost demonic tone. "I'm still your father, and will always love you, but if you ever tell Shelia that, I'll kill you."

He puts Tip down and backs up. "Now get the fuck out my house and don't come back until you've come to your damn senses and know your place again."

For the next six years the only time Tip came to his parents' home was when his father wasn't there.

Gerald, Ramon and Trey are all staring at and listening to Tip. When he's silent for a few minutes too many, Gerald says, "Well, what was it? Don't leave us hanging, man. Finish the story."

"You know what, Gerald; I think my drinking increased when I decided to start being your big brother for real." He looks over at the liquor cabinet. "Shit, I could use a drink right now."

"Tip," Gerald shouts. "Stop ho-humming and spill it."

"Yeah," Trey interjects, "and did you ever tell grandma?"

Tip turns to Ramon. "First, I want to thank you for going through all you did to get Little Tip back here. There's nothing I can do to repay you, but"—he pushes the manila envelope over to Ramon—"I hope this will help in what you're seeking to accomplish today."

Ramon pulls the one sheet of paper in the envelope out. After he reads what's on it, his mouth gets dry and he looks at Gerald.

"What?" Gerald asks. "Will one of you tell me what's going on?"

Ramon hands him the sheet of paper. "It's my birth certificate."

Gerald peruses the information on the certificate from top to bottom, and then he and Ramon look at Tip again.

"Is this real?" Ramon asks.

"Yes," Tip answers. "Dad may have said Mother Shelia forgave all his sins, but for some reason he must've felt her knowing he had two children by other women, instead of just one, was something she wouldn't be able to handle. I didn't find out much about your mother, other than where she lived, but apparently dad had some bogus adoption papers drawn up because there aren't any on file anywhere."

"Wait," Gerald says, with a conflicted tone. "Are you telling us Ramon is dad's . . .?"

"Biological son." They all jump a little at hearing Claudette's voice. She's standing in the door to the kitchen. She comes to the side of the table where Ramon is and sits beside him.

"You're Tip's mother?" he asks.

"Yes, but don't hold that against me, young man." Claudette winks at Tip then places her hands on the sides of Ramon's face and gazes into his eyes as if she's searching for something within him.

"You are his son, Ramon. Gerald Sr. may have kept secrets from Shelia, but he chose to reveal it all to me. This is a lot today, not just for the rest of the family, but you too. See, I'm an old woman now and we see things beyond regret and anger. When you've been on the earth 77 years like me, those two emotions have been kicked to the curve a long time ago.

"Now, Gerald Jr." She blows a kiss at Gerald. "You better get rid of them too, especially all that you're mad about. I saw and heard all that ruckus in the front room earlier, don't think I didn't. Y'all never know where I am." She laughs.

"The Lord left me here this long for a reason; he knew this day was coming and y'all need some mama love to get you through it. While y'all were still acting up out in the living room, humph, I got in my car drove around the corner and dug that envelope up from my old boxes at the house. It's time for y'all boys to come together as one."

"All this is unbelievable," Ramon says with a pained expression. "He was my real father; I don't understand why he didn't tell me that."

"Big Pa, I'm ready to eat more." Lia walks in the room rubbing her eyes. She goes over and raises her arms up to Gerald and he puts her in his lap.

Ramon stares at Lia mesmerized. His eyes get watery again. He's only seen her from afar.

She gives Ramon the onceover and says, "Hi, my name is Lia, what's yours?"

Ramon is speechless.

"I think you should answer her," Bridget says as she and Camilla walk into the kitchen arm in arm.

Ramon clears his throat. "My name is Ramon." He can't take his eyes off Lia.

She puts her hand out to him. "Nice to meetcha," she says.

Ramon looks at Gerald, who nods his head. He then puts his hand on top of Lia's, and gives it a light squeeze. "It's really nice to meet you, young lady. You're so beautiful."

"Thank you very much, and you know what?"

"No, please tell me," Ramon answers.

Lia smiles when she says, "You have the same eyes like my mommy, but she in heaven now."

Everyone stops moving as once again in a two week period the Lamar family is left without a dry eye in the room.

"I need to get some air." Gerald stands and puts Lia down beside Camilla, then walks out of the side door off the kitchen. He stands in the backyard viewing the sprawling estate his parents left him. His mind is in complete overload. "God, please don't cast me away from You; restore unto me a right spirit," he prays.

Then he hears, "I am your blood brother . . . I will never ever leave you nor forsake you again. Not even for a girl."

Gerald turns around and he and Ramon stand face to face both with wet bloodshot eyes. Together they proclaim once more—almost on the same spot they did as children, "Especially not even for a stupid ole girl." They hug and wrap their arms around each other, relieved to rid their minds and hearts of a longing that's held them hostage for over nine years.

*If you enjoy her novels please read the following excerpt from Mary Finley's next release: **All Right At The Same Time.***

"Hell found me!" Mary Ann Lewis finally reached the top of a steep hill. "This has got to be one of the worse days in my entire life."

She sat down on the hot, metal seat at the bus stop, and glanced over at the flashing sign on the bank across the street. "One hundred and twelve damn degrees, yes, hell has definitely found me."

She hated Dallas in the summer. It wasn't her idea to move there anyway. *Why did I let him talk me into this? Now he's let me down again for the millionth time.* She didn't know where her husband, Ray, was and didn't give a damn.

She fanned her face with a newspaper and sweated bullets, remembering the humiliation of having her car repossessed, right from the parking lot at her job. *Yeah, I put his ass out, sure did. Got me walking up this freaking hill, to catch the no. 3 bus on my first day at a new job.* She closed her eyes and took a deep breath.

This time I'm really getting a divorce; I've had enough. Mary Ann felt tears welling up. She turned, looked back down the hill and rolled her eyes. Her neighbor, Mrs. Lorraine Barrett, was swiftly making her way up. Mary Ann shook her head. *Now that's the last thing I need, this old biddy sitting with me while I wait on the bus. She better not say anything crazy to me or I'll curse her flat out. She does not need to activate me today!*

Mrs. Lorraine smiled when she reached the bus stop, "Good afternoon, young lady. Oh, ain't this a blessed day?"

"If you say so, Mrs. Lorraine." Mary Ann put on a plastic smile. "You doing all right today I see."

"Yes, well you know what today is, don't you?"

"No, is this a special day for you?"

"I'm on my way to see George."

Mary Ann raised her eyebrows. *Lord, this woman's husband been dead for over 20 years.*

Mrs. Lorraine chuckled as if she was reading Mary Ann's thoughts.

"I know you're probably wondering if I done lost my mind, but I'm on my way to the cemetery, haven't missed one Memorial day ride there since my wonderful George left me. My daughter gets off

195

work too late, so I climb this rugged hill this day, every year." She turned and put her hand on Mary Ann's shoulder. "Look at me, child."

Mary Ann took another deep breath, and stared at Mrs. Lorraine. *Ok, here it comes. She lives right under me and Ray so I know she heard the fight last night. Why me, Lord?*

"I'm not going to judge you. Listen, I know what folks in the apartment complex think about me. I'm the old, senile widow that's always in everybody's business. Well, I'll have you know, I'm a very caring person. I care a lot about you. You and Ray have helped me so much. Taking me to the grocery store, watching my place when I'm out, and giving me rides to church. Both of ya'll such good children. You just young that's all."

"I appreciate what you're trying to say, but . . ."

"How you gone appreciate it if I ain't said it yet?"

"I'm just not feeling very well. Maybe we can talk later when I get back from work." Mary Ann brushed back a tear.

"Child, you got to be patient with that man, you ain't been married but a little while. When me and George first got hitched, shoot I was leaving him going back to mama's almost every week. But I kept coming back because I loved him, and I knew he loved me." She pushed Mary Ann's bangs aside with her hand. "Do you love him?"

Mary Ann's cheeks were now stained with tears. "He's a good man. He doesn't cheat on me, and he always been faithful, from the first time we met. It's just that he can't keep a job. Seem like every other week he's quitting or getting fired."

"But if he's working, what does it matter if he gets a new job every day?"

"You're old school. It's different now days. Women don't put up with stuff from men like y'all did back then. I can't be standing by him no matter what. It's like the good times come so little now. Most times we're arguing more than loving. I mean what kind of man let's his wife lose her car?"

"Now, you can't believe he wanted that to happen, child. That's more of an embarrassment to him than you. Men have pride, baby, you young ladies these days just can't seem to stop stepping on a man's pride. All this talk about independence, that ain't how you

197

keep a man coming home. He has to feel needed."

"All I know is I'm climbing this hill, waiting on this bus in the scorching heat, why, because my husband didn't pay his part of the bills. When I needed him, he wasn't there. Hell, I think I'd be better off alone!"

Mary Ann put her head on the elderly woman's shoulder and wept. Mrs. Lorraine patted her on the back and gave her a handkerchief from her purse. "Listen." She lifted Mary Ann's chin with her index finger. "You didn't answer my question."

"What question?"

"Do you love him?"

Mary Ann wiped her eyes with her hands, stained them with mascara, and shook her head up and down. "So much, and he loves me too. I really don't want to leave him. He's trying. But why does it have to start so hard, you know this marriage thing. When does it get better?"

Mrs. Lorraine looked away, as if she was transported to another place and time. She was quiet for so long, Mary Ann got a little nervous. "Are you all right?"

Mrs. Lorraine stared into Mary Ann's eyes. Her voice was hoarse when she spoke again, "You know how me and George stayed married for 62 years?"

"How?" Mary Ann sat up attentively and waited for an answer.

"It's always sweet in the beginning. When the sweet goes sour, baby, if the love is strong enough, you just keep going, stay together, until the sweet comes back."

"It's not that easy, Mrs. Lorraine."

"Nobody said anything about easy, honey. You and that man are young, too young to understand, but if you give up now you never will." The bus Mrs. Lorraine was waiting on came to a screeching halt in front of them and she stood up.

Mary Ann stared with a confused look on her face. "Wait, Mrs. Lorraine, understand what? Please tell me."

—Full novel available the summer of 2017—

Made in the USA
San Bernardino, CA
14 March 2018